A Christmas Wedding
In Dixie

By

Beth Albright

Awards & Accolades for Author Beth Albright

DOUBLE Finalist for the **RT REVIEWERS** Awards

The Sassy Belles for *BEST CONTEMPORARY ROMANCE*

Wedding Belles for *BEST Contemporary Love and Laughter*

The Sassy Belles WINNER: *Best Debut Novel* from the *Book Junkie Choice Awards*

The Sassy Belles—
*Finalist BEST DEBUT NOVEL, RT REVIEWERS AWARDS, 2014
*Top Five Summer Pick – Deep South Magazine
*Finalist: Best Debut Novel – Book Junkie Choice Awards

Wedding Belles—
*Finalist BEST NOVEL, LOVE AND LAUGHTER, RT REVIEWERS AWARDS 2014
*RT Magazine Top Pick for August
*Nominated for GOLD SEAL OF EXCELLENCE, RT Magazine/August

Sleigh Belles—
*Barnes and Noble Bookseller Picks: September Top Pick for Romance

Praise For The Novels of Beth Albright

- Dripping with southern charm and colloquialisms, the novel once again proves Albright's firsthand knowledge of southern culture. *The women in Albright's novels are especially well written*—happy to challenge the status quo when necessary but also aware of that old adage, "You catch more flies with honey." This delightfully campy and romantic read will satisfy fans of Mary Kay Andrews, Alexandra Potter, and Lisa Jewell. **Booklist Review for** *Wedding Belles*

- *By turns tender, witty, steamy, and sharp, Albright's debut novel proves she's a gifted storyteller* with intimate knowledge of southern culture. This charming tale is tailor-made for fans of Mary Kay Andrews and Anne George." –**Booklist Review for** *The Sassy Belles*

- *…with distinct nods to the strength of family, the friendship sisterhood and the indomitable Southern spirit...Albright's first novel is a frothy, frolicking story...*" –**Kirkus Review for** *The Sassy Belles*

- *"Albright good-naturedly displays her inner redneck while steering this giddy Dixie romp with ease-leaving lots of room at the happy ending for another adventure starring these steel magnolias"* – **Publisher's Weekly Review for** *The Sassy Belles*

- "Readers will find some sexy, Southern fun for Christmas with The Sassy Belles." – Library Journal for *Sleigh Belles*

- *"The Sassy Belles are back and sassier than ever! ... With clever dialogue and richly drawn characters, Albright shows once again she's a natural-born storyteller who knows how to pen a charming tale.* Regardless of game-day colors worn, this sexy and fun Southern series will have readers coming back for more!" –**RT Magazine Review for** *Wedding Belles*

- *"The Sassy Belles reminded me that the South is like no other place on earth. Kudos to Beth Albright for capturing its spirit so perfectly in this lighthearted debut novel."* -Celia Rivenbark, New York Times bestselling author of *We're Just Like You, Only Prettier*

- *" Magic In Dixie serves up a heaping helping of Southern flavor and humor sure to please. Known for writing memorable characters with true southern voices and mannerisms, Albright ensures you don't have to be born in the south to appreciate the charm of her latest. So grab a box of Krispy Kreme doughnuts—you'll devour them as easily as this enjoyable summer read."* – RT BookReviews

- *"Beth Albright knocks it out of the ballpark with Christmas In Dixie. The characters are fun and full of life. What a great read!"*— BookMamaBlog

Other Novels By Beth Albright

In Dixie Series:

Magic In Dixie (Book One)

Christmas In Dixie (Book Two)

Daydreams In Dixie (Book Three)

Stardust in Dixie (Book Four)

The Sassy Belles Series:

The Sassy Belles

Wedding Belles

Sleigh Belles

Saved By The Belles

Memoirs

Southern Exposure; Tales From My Front Porch

Dedication:

To my Teddy, because I would do it all over again. Because you have such patience, even when I am pitching my Hissy Fits, even during the occasional all-out Conniption. Thank you for making me better. Thank you for making every single thing we do a team effort, from running errands to dreaming of new heights. Beside all the days since our sweetheart was born, my wedding day was my Best Day Ever. Because of YOU.

And

For my precious sweetheart, the best, most wonderful thing on earth, my Brooks—I love you always with my whole heart, so much I might burst. You are everything to me, forever and unconditionally. You are so strong and smart—I lean on you too much I'm sure. I am here for you always, no matter what—forever—we are a Teem.

To my "father" Richard J. Spavins—thank you for always believing in me. You never let me lose sight of all I am capable of, always there to push me forward. What would I have ever done without you in my life? I am so thankful to have you. I love you with all my heart.

And for my mother, Betty, my continuous inspiration and number one cheerleader. I love you. Because of you, I have become my dreams.

Chapter One

It was coming down in sheets, slapping at my windshield with heavy thuds. Freezing rain and ice covering everything in its path. It was a freak storm in Alabama. Even at Christmastime, temperatures usually hover around 50 degrees, sometimes even higher. The worst thing was—the entire week was supposed to be like this. Not good timing. The wedding was less than a week away and surely this awful weather would end long before Jack would lift my veil to kiss me—my first kiss as Mrs. Jack Bennett. A title I had dreamt of since I was just 14 years old. Okay, it had taken forever to finally get here but I was totally ready. If only this rain and ice would stop and we could get the temps a tad above 45 degrees I would be ecstatic. It was the Deep South after-all and we rarely had snow before late January. What am I talking about? We rarely had snow! Most of the time it was this stuff, wet and freezing rain as bloated and bruised gray skies would hang overhead, threatening more of the same, sometimes for days on end.

"For God's sake Rhonda, get your ass in here fast." One of my best friends, Vivi McFadden Heart was standing on the wide front porch of her centuries-old plantation home waving me inside as I pulled up to the front of her house, her gravel drive crunching beneath my tires. "We got work to do honey and the Fru Frus are already here."

"This weather couldn't be worse! I forgot about all this living in LA. Seventy-five and sunny 365 days a year!" I popped.

"Yeah well, I'm not there so it couldn't be *that* sunny!" She laughed, as I ran up the front steps dodging the frozen rain and slush.

Vivi gave me a tight quick hug and led me inside. My sisters, Abigail and Annabelle were already deep into conversation along with Blake, my other best friend, and the Fru Frus, our wedding planners. They own a Fru Fru Affair, and they are the best local event planners this side of the Mississippi. Coco and Jean-Pierre are warm and hilarious and totally perfect together. Both of them, men with their own unique style, were loud and gregarious and wonderful. They planned and coordinated Vivi's wedding and it was just spectacular. A tad over the top but suited Vivi to a T. CarolAnn, Annabelle's BFF, was also there, laughing along with all the other girls. It was a priceless moment, looking at them all together, crowded around the samples of fabric, color swatches and cake samples that the Fru Frus had delivered. With the wedding only days away, we had been running behind. All because of the crasher—yes—we had a possible wedding crasher and her name was Toots Harper Cartwright—better known as—Mother!

Two summers ago it had finally come out that she had been entangled in a life-long affair with my Daddy's brother—my uncle—Uncle Ron, who turned out to be my biological father. Yep, I am my sisters' first cousin, as well as their half sister. And people wonder how we southerner's get the reputation we do! Anyway, I moved from Los Angeles back home to Tuscaloosa to bury my poor daddy—who is actually my true uncle—are you following this—and after inheriting the dilapidated family home, I decided to stay here, renovate the old mansion and open a B&B in its place. I call it Southern Comforts.

When I was home to say goodbye to Daddy, and then got the upsetting news that he had left the old family home, a dilapidated haunted mansion, to me, I couldn't have been more angry. What did I want, let alone need, with the family home now in such shambles? After I got over my initial feelings of infuriation with Daddy for doing this to me, I realized I could make it work, renovate our home, and maybe do some good for my family. It's been two years now, and the Southern Comforts Inn is a Tuscaloosa treasure. We are booked solid most of the year.

But, the very best part of moving back to Tuscaloosa was finding my Jack. He was the first boy I ever kissed. I was only fourteen years old. Not long after Jack and I became serious, my younger sisters, who are twins but look nothing alike, met the loves of their life too and now we have a triple Christmas wedding planned. At 7pm on Christmas Eve, we will all get married at the Inn, which is right where we all grew up. It's exciting and we are all a bit of a nervous wreck. But doing this together makes it even more special. And with Blake and Vivi, my long lost best friends from childhood, and my sisters, this is seriously the very best time of our lives— but then Mother decided she wanted to be in the wedding too. That was hard enough, considering that she had kept her affair, and therefore my true lineage, a secret for over thirty years. But we all agreed, she was still our mother and sure, okay, she could be one of our bridesmaids, throw a shower, anything to make her happy.

Only it didn't. Nothing any of us came up with made her even smile. No. She wouldn't take us up on any of the things we suggested, from serving punch at the reception to us lighting a special candle for her and daddy and Granny Cartwright. Then we offered her the best we had—to be a bridesmaid. We were all shocked when she turned it down too! I mean, normally the mother is not a bridesmaid too! But Toots had always done things her own way. And the worst part, at least for the three of us, is that she wanted things her way—all the time. Mother Toots wanted one thing and one thing only from this wedding. And she wasn't fixin' to back down either.

She wanted to be one of the brides!

Chapter Two

"Hey Girlie, get in here and give us a hug," Coco oozed. He stretched his long thin arms toward me and pulled me into his chest. "Lord honey, you are soakin' wet. Don't drip all over the samples," he grinned.

"Hey honey, I can't even believe we are less than a week away," Blake reminded. She stood up to hug me.

"I sure hope this cold rain stops, my hair will be a frizzy mess," Annabelle prissed as she smoothed her hair.

"I know it, not to mention the vintage dresses Sugar Jones is making and red velvet capes I've had ordered," CarolAnn said. "The capes are arriving today. I've got Sugar Jones waiting at the store for them."

CarolAnn owned a vintage dress shop downtown and she and Sugar were in charge of the attire for the ceremony. Sugar Jones was the daughter of Sweetie Pie Jones, the best seamstress in town. She had made Vivi's wedding dress all by hand. Sugar was just like her mother but really into vintage and she had become the go-to designer for wedding gowns. She could make or fix anything. CarolAnn hired her on the spot when she found out she was Sweetie-Pie's girl. I couldn't wait to see her creations!

"A lady can't live on sweets alone, now, y'all c'mon in here to the kitchen and get yourselves some lunch," Arthur demanded. He was Vivi's African American cousin, and the man who ran her large home, as he had for years before they found out they had an Uncle issue just like me—ahem.

"Yes y'all, get on in here and try this new sauce Arthur's been working on. He's outdone himself I'd say!" Bonita, Arthur's wife, waddled into the room, very pregnant, and smiled her big warm grin at us, motioning us all to Vivi's kitchen.

Arthur had married the lead detective of the Tuscaloosa Police Department, a larger than life African American, doll-faced, plus sized dynamo named Bonita. I never met anyone smarter. She was quick, sassy and beautiful and she loved Arthur fiercely. They were great together. She was helping him work on all the food, good ol' southern BBQ and ribs for the reception dinner. They had opened a BBQ place on the property and it was the talk of the town. But Bonita was nine months pregnant and ready to give birth at any moment. She kept saying all the babies in her family were always late and she knew this baby, a girl, would be running late like every other female in the family. Though we laughed, I was a bit nervous. Bonita was a big woman and she looked like she was giving birth to triplets. *One more week*, I kept telling myself.

"One week y'all and you'll be married! Honeymoons and Christmas—sounds like perfection to me," Blake bubbled.

"I know it, the thought of it hits me and makes my head spin," Abby chimed. "Oh to finally be married to Ben is a dream come true."

"Then why didn't you take him up on the invitation the first time?" Vivi chortled.

"I was an idiot," Abby affirmed. "No two ways about it. I had no idea who I even was back then. It was so long ago and I'm just so happy he let me have another chance. He never gave up—never let go. He's the most romantic man I've ever met."

"I beg your pardon, I am marrying the most romantic man in Tuscaloosa," Annie countered. "Matt is the hottest, sexiest hunk T-Town has ever seen. I mean he *is* a mountain climber after-all."

"Honey, I got y'all both beat—Jack is a former Heisman winner, Bama football star. I have the sexiest man in town, hands down," I boasted.

Blake and Vivi glanced at each other. Surely they thought they had already won this contest years ago. Blake's hubby was the Tuscaloosa Chief Of Police and former football star, Sonny Bartholomew, And Vivi was married to the Play- By- Play announcer for the Crimson Tide, Lewis Heart, Blake's ex-brother in law. Like I mentioned earlier-we keep it all in the family—the in-laws, and the outlaws, down here in the Deep South.

"It sure looks like we are all set," I declared. "We have the cakes, the dresses and capes, the bridesmaid's dresses, all the flowers, and the orchestra. Now if I could only breathe."

"Honey we got you," Coco promised. "It's all good. Just relax. It's under control."

"Yes, Sugar, listen to him. You ladies just take it easy. Just show up and say 'I do.'" Jean-Pierre agreed.

But the prickly feeling I had gnawing away at the pit of my stomach was incessant. It ate away at me day and night. It was an uneasiness—because I knew my mother better than anyone. I was older than my sisters and I remember all too well how sneaky she could be. How she slipped out of our house in the wee hours, how she stretched the coiled phone chord into the kitchen pantry for privacy, keeping the light off to have her midnight phone conversations, the whispered tones floating out from the levered doors, along with her cigarette smoke. My sisters were fast asleep. But I was awake in bed, feeling this familiar gnawing I felt right now. I had been feeling it all my life.

Just then, I heard the gravel crunch in the driveway of

Vivi's house.

"Oh that'll be Sonny. He's taking me out to see Meridee tonight," Blake said as she stood from the big kitchen table to get her coat. "Meridee is needing a bit of help for her big Christmas dinner. She's having it a day early this year so she can be with us all at the wedding. We got rum balls to make tonight!"

"Anything with balls!" Vivi giggled. "Just the way it oughta be. Women are always in charge of the balls!"

Vivi followed Blake into the grand hallway to see her out.

"You're never gonna change my dear, and good thing," Blake laughed, "you keep us all on top of things, so to speak."

"Yep, we have to stay on top of our balls, that's for sure!" Then Vivi abruptly stopped laughing. "Oh God, y'all get in here—you ain't gonna believe who's in my driveway."

"You mean it's not Sonny?" Blake blurted as Vivi shoved her back inside.

"Not unless he's recently gotten a thing for high heels," Vivi quipped.

We all jumped up and trotted from the kitchen to the front windows and peered out into the freezing rain. Fog was creeping in slowly like a ghost hovering over-ground through the thick wooded lawn as the early evening began to blanket the frozen barren landscape outside. But even through the thick grey mist I could see the tall brunette in the pencil skirt and sweater. It was Mother and she was here to claim her place.

Chapter Three

We all stood at the window, peering out at Toots as she made her way through the cold and fog to the front porch of Vivi's house.

"Hey y'all," she chirped as she came through the front door.

Blake dropped her coat over the settee and moved over to hug her, fake grin and all.

"Hey Mother Toots, good to see you. We were just wrapping up," Blake offered.

"Yes, well I'm so glad I caught y'all before everyone left. I needed to talk to my girls if I could," she whined.

Oh God, here it comes, we are less than a week away and she was relentless. "Okay," I said approaching her, "Here we are. What did you need?" I asked bluntly.

"Can I see y'all privately?" She questioned with a serious look in her big blue eyes. Toots could sweet talk her way into anything. I knew we were in for a tiring discussion. But Abby and Annie and I had already discussed this, numerous times. We all felt the same way; Mother had caused us enough trouble with all of her sneaking around and lies and questionable behavior. We had dealt with her all of our lives, controlling everyone and demanding things from everyone in the family, constantly pushing to get her way. But not this time. This was our wedding for heavens sake! But I knew her tenacity and she wasn't going to back down. She had an affair with my uncle. It was simple to me. She stole the only father I had ever known, and heaved chaos into all of our lives as if she were puffing smoke from her signature long cigarettes. Had she shown any care or concern for daddy? Or me? Or my sisters? No not even once. Oh, we had talked about it. Hell we had even forgiven her. But now this was just too much. Forgiveness didn't mean I would ever be able to forget. How could I?

"Girls please, may we speak in private?" Mother Toots urged. Annie rolled her eyes as we all headed further down the front hall all the way back under the ornate curved staircase. I felt my stomach twist as Abby grabbed my hand and squeezed. I shot them both a look as we gathered into a tight little circle, the four of us, with Blake and Vivi just out of ear-shot. I raised my eyebrows at her, awaiting her never-ending plea.

"Listen to me, please. I am begging you. Nothing would make me happier than to share this experience with the three of you," she began. "I know how you all must feel but this would be the perfect way to end all this for good."

"End what Mother? End your guilt?" I pushed.

"No, I mean, well, in a way," she droned. "It just lets me know that Ron and I will be part of your lives, that everything is okay now."

"Seriously? You think that getting married at our wedding, and I say *OUR* wedding because it is ours not yours—you think that means it's all peachy and sweet and we can all be one big happy family now? I mean Mother— because of you I have sister-cousins!! We're like the trashy white folks people make fun of. And you did this. I have forgiven you, I have made peace with it, but please, this is my wedding day. Mine! And Abby's and Annie's. Ours. I'm sorry but you need to think about what you're asking. I can't do it. I don't know about them but I can't." I gestured to my sisters and shook my head.

"Abby, come on. I have been a good mother and nothing would mean more to me than to share this day as new beginning for all of us." Mother pressed. "Please?"

Abby shook her head, arms folded.

"Annie, you've got to know I never meant to hurt you girls. You were and are my whole world."

"Were we Mother? Really?" Annie jumped in. "I know you worked hard for us and kept us all together as best you could but much of our childhood distress came from your actions with Uncle Ron," Annie surmised.

"We were miserable all the time because though we didn't know what was happening but we knew *something* was going on. We knew things were bad between you and Daddy. But what you were doing behind our backs made it all so hard for us," Abby added.

" I'm so sorry but you know I meant well. No mother is perfect. Whatdya say? Please let me share in this day with y'all. It would mean the world to me."

Just then I felt Annie's hand slip into mine, and I slipped mine into Abby's. We were united. A front of sisterhood.

I spoke first.

"Mother we love you very much. You were good and did what you could but we all feel like this is our day and we don't want to add any other brides. *We* are the brides marrying the love of our lives. We want to keep it that way. I'm sorry." I tried to be to-the-point and strong.

"I can't believe you three!" Mother huffed like she did when she didn't get her way. "Ron is and always has been the love of my life too," she muttered. "You'll never understand. Maybe you are all more like your father than I thought."

"You mean me? Uncle Ron, the love of your life IS my father!" I snapped.

"No, them," she said with a gesture to my sisters. "He

never understood me either."

"Poor Daddy, I guess he wouldn't have—he never understood how in the hell you could be married to him and screwing his brother, then having a child, acting like it was his and ruing the lives of five people at one time!" Abby became incensed. "So Yes, I guess we *are* just like him— Good at living with our heads buried."

Mother glared at Abby then wiped a tear from her cheek and abruptly turned and left, her heels clicking down the hardwood floor. "Thank you Vivi. Y'all have a nice evening," she said as she headed back into the bitter-cold night air.

I began to cry and my sisters soon followed. It was so hard. She was our mother and our love for her was deep and unconditional but a wedding day—well that is special and none of us felt we wanted her and my uncle-daddy to be married right along-side us. "Oh Blake, I feel awful," I said barely able to speak as I wiped away the heavy tears. "I just—I just,"

Blake interrupted. "It's okay. It's totally understandable. Y'all all need to come sit here and listen to me." She reached out for our hands with both of hers and Vivi reached for us all too. "Sit here," she said softly leading us to the antique yellow settee in the grand front hall. "I just know your mother will come around. She knows deep down that your weddings that night are yours alone. Eventually she will be happy for you. I promise." I caught a knowing glint in her eyes. Was she up to something? Blake was an attorney—one of the best in town. What was she thinking?

"I hope so," I muttered. "I mean I don't want any more hurt in this family. We have all been through enough, especially the last couple of years," I responded. "I mean with the death of Daddy, having to decide what to do with that haunted mansion he left me, then re-doing the whole thing, opening the Inn and falling in love with Jack—well that was what saved me in all of this," I sighed. "Falling in love with my Jack."

"And that is your focus," Blake reminded sternly. You

and Jack. And you and Ben and You and Matt," she said as she looked each of my sisters and me in the eyes. "You're all getting married for heaven's sake! Now stop crying and get it together and act like the princess brides you are."

"Yeah or we may have to eat all this cake ourselves!" Vivi belched with a grin.

"And honey, Lord knows I can't carry no more weight. I'm 'bout to blow as it is," Bonita popped.

"Y'all don't have a thing to cry about," Coco shot. "Your mother is pulling a bride-zilla. I'm your wedding coordinator and what I say goes. This wedding is for three brides only. We can't fit another dress down that stairway, especially with those huge red capes CarolAnn ordered. Someone will go over the side for sure!"

"So true," Jean- Pierre added. "Plus one more wedding cake and I swear we will all die in a diabetic coma. Four brides and one priest is like a wedding deal at Sam's Club y'all. A big-box wedding has no class. And seriously, I don't do weddings in bulk. Three is my limit." He rolled his eyes and brushed his nails along his navy velvet jacket. "Plus your mother may I say, just isn't quite as classy as y'all. I'm already worried she's gonna walk around the reception eating the cheese-ball like it's an apple!"

We all laughed. It was always the way we handled any crisis, any sadness—eventually we laughed. And on that frigid late-December night in the warmth of Vivi's home, we laughed together.

We heard the gravel crunch as Mother backed her car out and the sounds of the car engine fade as she turned out onto the paved street at the end of Vivi's long drive.

"It's all gonna be okay. Always is," Arthur assured as he brought us our coats. "You'll see."

He was an averaged sized man but his heart was warm and big like a full moon. It glowed with care and love. He was one of the most wonderful human beings I had ever known. He was just the same when I used to come to Vivi's to play as a child. He is a caretaker. There are just people like that—who love to care for others. Bonita was one lucky woman. They weren't just a married couple. They were one of those couples who truly became one. Arthur was soothing. And it was just what we needed.

We all stood in Vivi's grand hall and were slipping into our coats and hugging goodbye when headlights flashed in the front windows. It had gotten late and the cold air had a bite. When mother opened the front door, the frost and freezing rain had blown inside and exaggerated the chill she had left in her wake.

"Who the hell could that be on a Sunday night at this hour?" Vivi yelped. "This damn place is turning into Grand Central!"

We all peered out the frosty milk glass windows. The old model light blue Chevy Impala rolled to a stop. The clicking and knocking of the engine continued after the car had been turned off and a billowing cloud of gray smoke escaped from the old muffler. A tall shadow in a long coat appeared and ran up the front porch stairs, the beehive hairdo sparkled with ice crystals as the night skies continued to spit freezing rain.

"Oh My God!" Blake shouted.

"What? Who is it?" Abby interjected.

"Lord have mercy," Vivi gasped "What in the hell is she doing here? This can't be good. It's never good when she shows up."

"Who is that lady? And that outfit—caftans went out with lava lamps," Annie gibed.

"I can't believe she's here. She must've had a bad vision," Blake suggested. "Something we all need to know—

"And obviously, it couldn't wait," Vivi interrupted.

The doorbell rang and Vivi flung open the huge door. There standing in the cold of late December, shivering, arms folded was Myra-Jean, the trailer-park psychic. Lord help us.

Chapter Four

"Get in here, honey. What the hell brings you out on a night like this?"

Vivi led her inside.

"Y'all, I had to see you!" Myra-Jean burst. "I had a vision during the ice-storm today and I had to tell you." Myra-Jean was breathing hard and heavy. She had a wild look in her eyes. It really made me nervous, almost scared. I barely remembered Myra-Jean. Mother Toots and Blake's Mother, Kitty, used to go see her when Blake and I were little girls. She had always been a bit of a joke in town, but people went to her for fun. Except Mother. She put stock in everything Myra-Jean told her. She would burn sage to rid the house of bad spirits, and bring Myra-Jean to the house for "emergency readings" and other frantic fits where one might need a psychic.

"How did you know where we were?" Blake asked.

Of course I wanted her to say, "I'm a psychic, I always know where y'all are." But she just stood there shaking her head.

"It doesn't matter, I'm just so glad I found y'all. I have to tell you—I had a vision, and y'all need to know, this here wedding is in trouble. I see something awful happening. Just awful."

"What?" Annie exclaimed. "What is it? Is Matt okay?"

"Oh honey, it's everybody," Myra-Jean informed. "All of y'all are in danger. I see danger that night. Just pure ol' dee danger. I can't quite make it out but something's gonna happen."

"Y'all this is scaring me," Annie said.

"Me too and I don't even believe in all this stuff," Abby agreed.

"Do we need to change the date or the location or what?" Annie continued nervously.

"Wait wait wait!" I demanded. "We're less than a week away and we aren't changing a thing! This is totally ridiculous!"

"Now Myra-Jean, you know we love you but it's too late," Blake assured. "They begin decorating the house tomorrow. Everything is already in motion."

Myra-Jean put the back of hand to her forehead dramatically and plopped onto the settee. She shook her head. The color left her cheeks and she became pale.

"Get her some water Coco, she looks like she's gonna faint," Vivi ordered as she sat down next to her and put her arm around her. "We're getting some water, honey. Just take a deep breath, okay?"

"I need y'all to take me seriously. I know what I feel. It's the most ominous thing I ever felt."

"Okay, sugar, here's some water. Drink up. I wanna hear this," Coco urged as he delivered the icy beverage and scooched in next to Vivi. He had always believed in Myra-Jean's 'visions'. We all gathered around Myra-Jean like we were fixin' to hear a ghost story. She took a big gulp of water and dabbed her lips with the billowy sleeve of her caftan.

"I'm tellin' y'all, you gotta change this weddin'. That's all I know."

"Okay wait, so not only are we having the whole "Sam's Club" style wedding in bulk, now we're gonna listen to a tall redhead in a paisley caftan tell us a week out that we gotta change everything 'cause the spirits told her we're in danger? The only danger I'm in is this nightmare I'm livin' right now. Girl, I can feel my reputation turning to crap right in front of me!" Jean-Pierre ranted with exasperation in his voice.

We all stood there first looking at Myra-Jean, then at each other. Could it be true? Was there an aura hanging over us—a cloud of darkness? Then Vivi interrupted the brief silence.

"No y'all, we need to listen to her. Remember when she did my reading before Lewis and I got married? She was right—something was wrong. She's good. We need to listen."

"Vivi," Blake reminded, "We were throwing you a wedding shower and she was a guest for fun, it wasn't supposed to be serious."

"Yes, but I was right, there was another woman, and you did have that beautiful red-headed baby girl. She does look just like you. I know what I saw in my vision." Myra-Jean took another swig and began to stand up. "Y'all just be careful," she warned as she headed toward the door handing Vivi her empty glass. "I've said what I came to say. Y'all can take it or leave it." Miss Myra-Jean stepped toward the door. Just as she reached for the handle she turned with a dire look in her eyes. "Blake and Vivi, y'all know me and you know my talents. I'm just here as the messenger. But remember, I warned y'all." And with that she was gone—as if on her broom.

A heavy silence fell over the group. I could hear Annie breathing next to me. I have to be honest—I was dumbfounded. Could she be right? Were we in danger? And from what? We stared at the front door as if someone else might pop through, another surprise guest. Oh, please not. I knew I couldn't take another unexpected visitor.

"Well I for one know she's right about her visions," Coco recalled. "Last time she saw a bunch of men in tight white pants for me and next thing you know, I was catering for the Nutcracker!"

Everyone burst out laughing just as the door slung open with Sonny and Lewis carrying their three year olds, Beau and Tallulah. Tallulah was Vivi and Lewis' little girl, all red headed ringlets and freckles with perfect emerald eyes just like her mother. Beau was Blake and Sonny's little boy, dark wavy hair and big blue eyes just like Blake. The men had taken the kids to a Christmas party for one of their pre-school friends.

"Well, you ladies look like y'all had a good day," Sonny said placing Beau down next to Tallulah. The two kids ran off giggling toward the kitchen with Bonita. "How many mojitos y'all have?"

"I'll have you know we barely drank," Vivi popped. "We had too much to do. But it sure was a good day, interesting anyway."

"Okay, I know that look," Lewis observed. "What really happened here? Annie here looks like she just saw a ghost."

Lewis was good. He could read anybody and he knew Abby and Annie well. They both worked for him at his radio station. He stood looking around the room, taking in the laughter covering the uneasiness of the last few minutes. Myra-Jean had cast a shadow over the wedding in her five-minute visit and we all were still feeling the moment. Lewis knew it. But no one wanted to say anything. I mean we had two women fly in on their brooms in the last half hour— Myra-Jean and Toots Cartwright. It was enough to make us all need a Rolaids chaser to the cake and mojitos.

"I'll fill you in later. My girls are fixin' to leave and I need some hugs goodbye," Vivi announced.

We all began to walk out into the cold night, Lewis headed to the kitchen to check on the kids as Sonny followed shooting Blake a puzzled look. I followed Abby and Annie out onto the porch and slid on my white fuzzy mittens. Blake hugged Vivi and came out last, Vivi stepping out onto the porch in her dress and apron. She folded her arms tightly and shivered in the frigid chill, "Y'all get out of this weather now, drive safe. And don't worry. It all turns out fine—it always does. I love y'all. Night." Blake stopped to slip on her crimson leather gloves. "Love you right back honey. I'll call you in the morning." Vivi closed the door. Coco and Jean-Pierre hugged us and headed to their car, the freezing rain still falling, looking like tiny diamonds dripping steadily under the amber driveway light.

"What do you make of this?" I asked her as we made our way to our cars.

"I'm not sure but I think something's going on. Maybe I can fish around and see if anyone knows something we don't. I do know one thing," she promised, "I'm not gonna let this just sit here. Maybe she just wanted her fifteen minutes you know? She can be a bit dramatic." Blake smiled but I could tell in her eyes she was full of questions. Sonny came through the door with Beau on his hip and slipped his arm around Blake's waist.

"Ready?" He asked.

"Yep, let's go home." Blake smiled and linked her arm into his as they descended the steps and headed to her car. I stood there watching Abby and Annie get into theirs and as everyone left I stood among the falling frozen crystals and breathed in the crisp cold night. No matter what, I knew it would be okay. I was finally marrying Jack, and that was all that mattered. I knew that but still, between Myra-Jean and Mother Toots, having this wedding go off without a hitch would take a Christmas miracle. Maybe I would play it safe and just ask Miss Myra to sprinkle some of that sage over the alter. Just in case.

Chapter Five

The sunlight splashed against the wood floor of my bedroom. The cool gray skies and freezing rain had taken a respite and the morning light peeked from behind the pink-tinged silver-lined clouds. The light coffee-colored walls warmed the room, pale dusty pink curtains pooled on the floor framing the floor to ceiling windows. It was a soft beginning to what I knew would be a hectic day.

The families would all begin arriving at the Inn tomorrow. Jack's family from their beach house, where they now lived on the Gulf Coast, Ben's family from North Alabama, and Matt's father from New York. His mother had passed away a few years ago. I had heard Matt's dad was a bit eccentric so I was intrigued.

I laid still in the quiet of the morning, Jack sleeping soundly beside me. He was one of those beautiful men, sandy hair, blue eyes, dimples, defined muscles and beautiful tanned skin even in the wintertime. Jack was the first boy I ever loved—the first boy I ever kissed and now, for the rest of my life, I would be able to kiss him anytime I wanted to. I wriggled down further into the bed burrowing a tad farther under the white down-filled covers. The warmth of his body next to mine was intoxicating—something I didn't want to end. I knew I had a million things to do but in that moment, I was right where I wanted to be, right next to Jack, in the warmth of our own bed, snuggled in on a cold December morning. It was heaven. I held on to it, looking at Jack as he slept—until my cell rang on my bedside table.

It was Blake. I knew whether I liked it or not, the day had started—"Good morning my dear," I answered trying to sound more awake than I was.

"Good morning sweetie. Hope it's not too early. Just wondering if I can see you for an early lunch today—I know it will be a hectic day with everyone arriving at the Inn tomorrow but I think you, and Vivi and I need to get together a plan—you know kind of a preemptive idea to make sure that between Toots and Miss Myra, we don't have the wedding fiasco of the year, know what I mean?"

I knew she was right and stronger together had to be the plan. That's the way we had always been. We had each other's backs. With both Blake and Vivi serving as my matrons of honor, I knew I needed them like never before. Not only was I a bride but, the Inn was hosting the event and the families of my sister's new husbands. My plate was overflowing.

"Absolutely! I agreed. "I don't want any surprises."

"Well I'm no miracle worker, honey but I'm trying. Okay I'll call Vivi and I'll see y'all at Noon. I can bring something and we can just meet there. Is that okay?"

"Oh yes, that sounds perfect. I have so much to do here and Jack is still working until tomorrow so he won't be here. It'll be just the three of us. I can fill in my sisters later tonight. I'll make the tea and coffee and y'all come on."

"One request—I need your special hot chocolate. The freezing rain may have stopped but it's like 20 degrees out here."

"Honey, I wouldn't know, I'm still in bed and Jack's

body is like a heater. I don't wanna move."

"Girl, don't get up until you have to," she laughed.

"Okay, see you in a few. Don't forget my hot chocolate." She hung up just as Jack opened his sleepy blue eyes and grinned at me.

"G'mornin' beautiful. How's my girl?"

I rolled over and kissed him as he slipped his arm beneath my waist and pulled me into him. Jack was shirtless, and his soft skin was warm and smooth and he cradled me into his chest, caressing his fingers through my hair.

"Just hold me before we have to get going. This day is gonna be crazy." I pushed in closer to him.

"It's gonna be fine—you have lots of help coming to finish up all the work. All you have to do is tell them what you want. By tonight the place will be beautiful, covered in Christmas decorations, and the house will be cleaned and ready for everyone. I promise, all you need to do is think about marrying me. In just a few days, you will be mine forever, and you will make all my dreams come true. Nothing else really matters." He kissed me softly then pulled back to look at my face.

"I love you Jack Bennett," I purred. I pressed my lips to his mouth and kissed him softly, my fingers travelling his body, down the side of his striped drawstring pajama pants, dipping down his backside inside his pants to squeeze his cheeks. I was filled with passion and love for this man. He was my rock. He was strong and solid. He had been so good in the crisis last Christmas with his ex-wife. It was during that time I learned what a fighter he is. He stood up for us and gave me the best Christmas of my life, asking me to marry him. He made me feel so loved and safe.

"I love you too, baby," he cooed. "You know I'm right; nothing else really matters. Take my hand—it's just us. The rest of this is just decorations. By the way, the surprise honeymoon is when all the real fun begins."

I was suddenly filled with a thrilling excitement. Our Honeymoon. I drew in a deep breath and kissed him again. I was suddenly filled with an energy I hadn't felt in days. Jack was right. It was just us. Nothing else really mattered. Everything I was worrying about would make it all prettier but really, the wedding was about the bond. And my sisters and I had the best. Once I stopped to think about it, it was the first time in such a long long time that we had all been happy, fulfilled and satisfied. We would all turn the page of our tumultuous past, our unpredictable childhoods and move into our own lives. It was officially over and now we could look forward to being wives, maybe even mothers. It was joyous. I kissed Jack one last time and jumped off of him.

"Blake is coming by for an early lunch, bringing goodies and Vivi. We're finalizing things," I said.

"See? Good! This day is going to be great. We can run back over your checklists when I get home," Jack assured. "I know you have about ten of them, but Baby I'm here to help. Remember, no matter what, the day is going to be great. It's you and me, Christmas Eve, got it?" Jack lifted my chin with his index finger and looked deeply into my eyes, as if to reassure this promise.

"It's a date baby," I purred. "Spending Christmas morning with you as my husband, then zooming off to someplace wonderful—I have to pinch myself. It feels like a dream." I left the bed and prissed to the closet, flinging open the doors. "Last day before everyone we love is all under one roof," I reminded.

"And no matter what, it's all gonna be fine," Jack offered. But, somehow that ended with the slight sound of a warning. I smiled at him and stepped into my closet as Jack headed toward the bathroom. I heard the steam shower come on. I had to keep telling myself it would all be fine. No matter what happens, no matter who shows up, whatever surprises, we would be Mr. and Mrs. Bennett in a few short days. Jack was so easy-going. He was the steady ship to my chaotic, frantic nature. Just what I needed. I got dressed in a hurry. Coco and Jean-Pierre were coming at nine o'clock. I had blackberry scones and orange muffins ready to throw in the oven. I had to get the hot chocolate going for Blake.

I scurried around the house lighting all the fireplaces. Garlands of red holly and evergreens hung over each mantel in swags, and the fragrance floated throughout the mansion. The twenty-foot Noble fir tree stood elegantly in the curve of the banister of the front hall staircase. Tiny amber lights glittered the evergreens and the holly that hung in scalloped drapery up the original stairs. It would be where my sisters and I would descend into the arms of our men in just a few days. The Fru Frus were coming by to check the lists and make sure all the food and essentials were in place for delivery. They also had the daunting task to complete the decorating for the grand hallways, the left parlor where the actual ceremony would take place and the huge ballroom that we used as a game and football Saturday room. Our guests who weren't going to the game in the fall loved hanging out in the huge room, all the big screens on the Crimson Tide. We had a nice bar in there and it was going to be absolutely perfect for the reception.

The entire house, and all the food, decorations and linens must be ready and in place by the next morning for all the arriving family. Jack's family was due to arrive first. I had only met them once. His mother was a tiny blonde, a bit pretentious and always in perfect clothes and very stiff hair. His dad was gregarious and out-going but usually half a sheet to the wind—probably to fortify himself to put up with his wife. Eleanor and Jack Sr. would surely give me a run for my money. I could bet she would walk through the house with a fine-toothed comb and he would be asking for a Scotch Neat the minute they got here. I had to stay focused. I had to make a mantra out of what Jack had reminded me. It would all be fine. It was all about us. Then suddenly it hit me—Jack's parents had never met Mother Toots! And oh my lord—what if Miss Myra-Jean shows up—the neurotic and the psychic— sounds like a horrible soap opera! I felt my stomach twist. *Breathe*, I told myself. Jack could take care of anything and he would. He was the steady ship—remember? He could calm me in any storm—even the ones named Hurricane Toots, Tropical Depression Eleanor and Tropical Storm Myra-Jean. And the first winter storm was rolling in here in less than twenty-four hours.

I knew I had to batten down the hatches.

Chapter Six

"Good morning Sugar! I decided to stop by The Waysider and grab us some ham biscuits," Blake announced as she clicked her heels across the wood floor of my foyer. I took her bag of biscuits as she dropped her coat on the hallway settee and we both headed toward the kitchen.

"I've got scones and muffins in the oven and fresh squeezed OJ in the fridge."

"Vivi's on the way," Blake continued as she sashayed past me and led the way into my cozy kitchen. "She went to the baby doc with Bonita this morning. I swear that lady's gonna pop before we know it!"

Blake took her seat at the red and white toile-covered banquette under the picture window. She looked amazing as usual, her long dark hair, shiny and bouncy, curved elegantly behind one ear. She had on a winter-white sweater and a single strand of pearls and her signature Ruby Woo blood-red lipstick from MAC. She was stunning, but down to earth and genuine.

"Okay honey tell me—you've got that 'I'm fixin' to be

hit by a train' look on your face. Or are you fixin' to throw up?"

"Oh it's nothing. I need to calm down," I explained. "I think I need a drink." I grinned as I opened the refrigerator door.

"Sugar! It's barely after 10:30 in the morning!"

"Well I can add a shot of vodka to this here OJ." She knew I wasn't serious but I wasn't convinced myself. I had a twinge in my stomach, a twist and an ache. This feeling was like a dark heavy quilt—like I knew this day wasn't about to go as planned.

"Tell me!" Blake demanded. "What is going on with you?"

I sauntered over with two glasses of orange juice and sat down next to her.

Just then we heard Vivi bound in the front door. "Where is everybody?" She bellowed. "I got us some Krispy Kremes."

"God, we're all gonna be too fat to fit into our dresses," I shook my head to Blake.

"Sounds perfect, she shouted, referring to the sugary doughnuts. "Get in here! We're already in the kitchen," Blake shouted to Vivi.

Vivi came in with the iconic green polka dot box and set it in the center of the table. I had gotten back up to hug her hello, then grabbed the OJ and poured her a glass of juice. I took the muffins and scones out of the warm oven and dumped them into a basket on top of a red checked cloth napkin. I brought over the butter dish and Vivi's juice, all on a tray of jams, and scooched in next to Vivi.

"Oh no, what's that look about?" Vivi asked with her copper eyebrow arched.

"I know it," Blake continued, "I have already asked her. So spill honey. That's what matrons of honor are for." Blake and Vivi were my matrons of honor together. My sisters and I had decided we would have a very small wedding party. Since there were three brides and we were getting married here in the house, we knew we needed a small party. Annie had CarolAnn as her maid of honor. Abby had asked Ben's sister to be hers. Ben asked his dad to be his best man, Jack had asked Lewis since they had known each other on the Bama football team and Matt had a surprise for us. An old friend of his from one of his climbs. Matt owned the new outdoor and camping store and had climb many of the world's tallest peeks. CarolAnn would be walking with the friend Matt was bringing. I was secretly kinda hopeful for CarolAnn. She had been alone for a long time and she was such a fun, warm woman. Annie had always been so close to her. She was like another sister. Just like Blake and Vivi.

I grabbed a Krispy Kreme and took a larger than usual bite. Both of the girls looked at me and smirked.

"You gotta fit into that dress sugar, so don't down too many of those," Blake advised.

"I've gotten so anxious that I can barely move. The other night I realized I was trying to lasso the TV remote with my phone cord. I'm immobile with my nerves on end," I confessed.

"You look like you could eat that entire box of doughnuts, honey. Come on, tell us what is swirlin' around in that head of yours," Vivi urged.

I took a swig of OJ like it actually was full of vodka, swallowed hard and looked at my oldest, dearest two friends.

"It's the hoidy toidy in-laws," I said. "The psychic from LaLa land, and toss in Mother Toots and you have a perfect storm for this Christmas wedding. I'm just a nervous wreck. The three of them together, and I just know something awful is gonna break out like a bad case of hives."

Both of them looked at me and shook their heads. "That's our job," Vivi explained. "We'll keep them all so busy, no one will have time to cause any trouble. Promise. Just leave it to us." They smiled at each other like they were about to play a prank on a teacher, or roll a yard on Halloween night.

I shoved another doughnut into my mouth as Vivi

reached for a scone and the butter. I felt a comfort come over me. Even though I knew they might have their own way of solving issues, I trusted them more than I trusted anyone. These two—these two strong, sassy, tenacious women had my back. All those years I had spent in LA I had been so lonely. I had a few friends but nearly everyone had a connection to my work. No one to just sit and talk to—like what I was doing at this moment. That loneliness was cold and prickly and I felt it every single day. It made me uneasy most of the time. Like my feet were never really on the solid ground. Yes, I knew I was homesick back then but I was far too stubborn to let it show. There were so many days I had wanted to just throw in the towel and get the hell out of the pressure cooker that is Los Angeles. But I kept going. That is until Daddy died and left me the haunted mansion here. Coming home was something I had thought about but never ever really planned on—too much water under the bridge here—too much pain. Too much Mother. She was difficult on her best days. Of course I knew she loved me deeply but she was always a hard pill to swallow.

All of it has turned out so well. Over the last year and a half, Mother has mellowed and things had fallen into place once I restored this old family home and opened my B&B, *Southern Comforts.* I had worked so hard to make it the success it had become. And Jack Bennett was a huge part of that. We were each other's first loves when we were barely teenagers and you know, you just never forget that first kiss—that first feeling of exhilaration, of warm, soft lips on yours—for the very first time—that strange heat stirring in the pits of your stomach. I never got over Jack. And he was right here waiting when I got home.

I heaved in a deep breath as I listened to Blake's deep rolling laughter warm up my Kitchen. She was that person that brought calm with her wherever she went. A feeling that no matter what, we could handle it together. The three of us had become The Sassy Belles back in middle school. She and Vivi continued our little club after my family moved away.

But we are all back together now and tighter than ever. I don't know what I would do without these two.

I laughed along with them as we filled our bellies with Waysider ham biscuits, Krispy Kremes and my home baked yummies. The kitchen was warm, though it was cold and Christmasy outside. I felt so safe. I knew I was in such a good place after so many years of loneliness. In that moment, as I looked at both of my dearest friends, my other sisters, I loved these women more than I ever had.

"Lord honey! You've outdone yourself!" Vivi bragged. "These scones are to die for. Hey! Have you ever thought about being a chef?" She laughed at her own joke. I had been a chef for as long as I could remember. I was in culinary school in LA.

"Hey I just had an idea," she continued as she spread more butter on her second blackberry scone. "You remember how Minnie in The Help was a cook too? Well we all know what kind of pie she baked for that lady who was driving her nuts and rude as hell—I'm not sayin' you should bake a shit pie for the wedding but if your mom and that psychic keep it up, well—you know."

"Vivi!" Blake yelped. "I am ashamed! Even for you that is pretty awful."

"What? Come on y'all...you never know just when you might need one of those pies."

I laughed at the thought of it. But it wasn't my mom I was thinking of when I thought of the shit pie Minnie baked. I hate to say it, but visions of Eleanor popped into my head. My soon-to-be-mother-in-law. She just had her head so far up her ass. She actually still had full-time maids at her house. And Jack had told me horror stories of how she treated them.

Just then the doorbell rang. I was sure it was the Fru Frus. They were running late. Time to finalize the home checklist for decorations. I jumped up and made my way to the door swishing over my hardwood floors in my fuzzy socks, my un-coifed morning hair pile on my head and secured with a clip. I was completely sans make-up. I wasn't too worried. It was morning and I was among friends. Hell my long chambray shirt was covered in stains from baking all morning. Without a second thought I flung open the door—only to find Eleanor and Jack Sr. standing there in the cold morning.

"Oh my goodness," I belted with my eyebrows arched, " I didn't expect y'all till tomorrow. That's when all the family is arriving. Come in! Come in!" I prodded.

My stomach dropped but I played gracious. I wasn't ready. The house hadn't been dusted. The bathrooms hadn't been scrubbed. I looked like a poor homeless woman. I was going into a deep silent panic, my stomach churning. Jack's mother was a woman of legend—not the good kind. More like a *Mommie Dearest*. Suddenly images of wire coat hangers filled my head and my heart sped up. I could feel it thumping in my throat.

Eleanor swished into my foyer first, followed by Jack Sr. He leaned in to kiss my cheek, my flour-covered cheek.

"Are you certain you're going to be ready, Rhonda?" They place looks a little underdone," Eleanor chided. "Ahem." She smirked and cleared her throat, and she had nothing in her mouth—except utter disappointment.

I'm a failure. Already.

Eleanor was a tiny underweight woman. Sharp pointed features, stiff blondish-gray hair, and a perfect tiny St. John knit dress. I was sure Eleanor didn't own anything that wasn't St. John in a size 2. She had a constant look on her face, a half frown, half smirk—no trace of a smile. No warmth. Ever. Just suspicion.

"Oh I'm not worried," I assured nervously. "I have my decorators coming and we have all of the items totally ready."

"Well, dear, let's hope they are bringing an army with them. You don't have a single thing up. I wouldn't even know it was Christmas."

I did have the tree and some lights, but for Eleanor, it could be an Easter tree.

"Hello, I don't think we've met," Blake said, entering

with her hand outstretched. "I'm Blake Bartholomew. One of Rhonda's best friends. We've been close forever. And you are?" Blake kept her hand outstretched in a greeting exuding more confidence than anyone I knew.

Blake was smooth. She was a high-powered successful attorney and it showed.

"I'm the mother of the groom," Eleanor popped back.

"Which one? We do have a triple wedding you know." Blake smiled.

"Yes, and whose grand idea was that?" Eleanor slithered.

"Mine," Blake snapped. "So whose mother are you?"

"Jack's. If you're Rhonda's best friend I'm sure you have heard of me by now. Eleanor Bennett."

"No. I can't say that I have."

Blake smiled knowingly.

"I sure hope you are here to help Rhonda get this place looking presentable." Eleanor stopped and gazed around the massive foyer, up the curved banister, to the twenty-foot ceilings.

"Oh, I'm not here to decorate. I'm here to make sure she has a fabulous wedding and no one brings her down or rains on her big day? Know what I mean?"

"Count me in for that one," Vivi rang out as she entered the room. "I'm Rhonda's other BFF, Vivi Heart. We're her matron's of honor and honey we've surely got her back. So don't you worry 'bout a thing," Vivi assured. "Hey Rhonda, didn't you tell me the in-laws weren't coming till tomorrow? Whatchy'all doin' here?" Vivi inquired.

Jack Sr. had left the little tete-ta-tete and wandered into the large parlor off the front entrance. Of course it was where the bar and booze were. He surely had a homing device. He'd have to in order to survive life with his tight-ass wife. He answered Vivi from the other room.

"Oh Elle just insisted we get here early to make sure everything was in order."

"Oh Jack, stop," Eleanor broke in. "I just wanted to see if you might need our help."

"Welp honey, that sure ain't no work outfit," Vivi pointed out.

"Yes, I do believe that St. Johns knit-wear might take a beating today. The decorators will be here soon and they just might put you to work. Better change clothes I think," Blake added with a sarcastic grin.

I sat there watching the fireworks and smiling to myself. I knew the rooms weren't ready. Sheets not yet on the beds. I had two helpers coming to clean and help serve, answer doors and take coats and Jean-Pierre and Coco would be doing all the decorating. By nightfall the place would be transformed. But now—Eleanor had no place to go. Unless I sent her up to her room dust and all.

All of a sudden the wind blew the front door open and there she stood, like a vision of horror in her paisley orange caftan, red hair wrapped in a pile of frizz and curls on top of her head. Myra-Jean had an announcement. "Girl's, y'all ain't gonna believe what I dreamed last night. This wedding's gonna be a nightmare, believe you me—y'all need to cancel. Now!"

Chapter Seven

I felt like I was swallowing my tongue. Jack Sr. peeked his head out from the side parlor. He had a drink in his hand. He had obviously helped himself to that Scotch Neat. Blake and Vivi looked at each other, then at me, shock in their eyes. I was speechless.

But of course Eleanor wasn't.

"Who the hell might this character be? Is she another of your bridesmaids, Rhonda?"

I moved at a clip to the front door, grabbing Myra-Jean by the forearm and turning her right around. Blake followed me.

"Oh honey - you must have the dates mixed up. That little brides-maids party is tomorrow. That's when you are supposed to perform your little show." I said it loud enough for nosey Eleanor to hear.

Blake took over and led her right back out into the cold December air. I smiled as Eleanor squinted at me over her shoulder.

"Oh, that's so funny," I fake-laughed. "She's just part of

the entertainment. You know she plays a psychic. It's all just for fun. The girls in the party are getting together tomorrow night for some fun. She must be a little confused."

"Let me go help Blake un-confuse her," Vivi offered as she scooted by Eleanor who was still blocking the front door, her mouth still dropped open at the whirlwind fiasco breaking out in my house. "I know that lady and she is known to get her days mixed up. 'Scuse me," Vivi pushed through, then looked at Eleanor, "and dear, you can close your mouth now."

I heaved in a deep breath as I stood with both my new in-laws.

"Well, I never," Eleanor snooted.

"Oh my God woman, of course you have," Jack shook his head. "Don't you remember that kook from down the street? You're always wanting to know what Shelby June thinks. Hell, you've paid her a fortune to read those damn cards."

"I have no earthly idea what you are speaking of, Jack. Now hush your mouth." Eleanor huffed as she drew her arms up and folded them across her chest. Suddenly I realized there was a public Eleanor, and a private Eleanor. And the private version obviously consulted psychics. Wonder what else she did in secret? She did seem like the kind of lady that might have some skeletons buried in her own closet. She certainly seemed taken off-guard with her husband's comment.

Blake opened the front door and came back inside, followed closely by Vivi. "Okay, she was just confused. Miss Myra will be back tomorrow." She smiled at me like she had just saved us from some embarrassment. And she had. She shot me a look that told me all I needed to know. Now, I thought, to get these two in-laws outta my house along with Miss Myra.

"Since you two have come a day early. I have a great idea! Why don't you go over to the campus and see the Bryant Museum? Jack's picture is there," I suggested.

"And my hubby's is too. Y'all know Lewis Heart is the

play- by- play announcer. Both he and Jack are featured there in the broadcast section. Y'all would love that," Vivi jumped in.

She tried to turn them and point them back out the door.

"Okay? Sound good?" Blake interrupted. "Maybe y'all can grab some lunch over at the Hotel Capstone. Y'all can follow me. I have a meeting on campus in twenty minutes," Blake pushed.

"Come on Eleanor. Let's get out of Rhonda's way. She's real busy. I told you we needed to wait until tomorrow but you never stop until you get what you want." Jack Sr. swigged the last of his Scotch. It wasn't even 11:00 in the morning and he was already drinking. I knew this was how he coped with his wife. Alcohol from sunrise to sunset. Jack obviously hadn't told me *everything* about his parents.

"Fine, but honey could you be a dear and make sure our rooms are ready by this afternoon?" Eleanor scoffed. "I am going to be just exhausted and will be looking forward to fresh sheets and linens. Oh, and I do hope we will have a room with our own claw-footed tub. It's what I have at home and my darling Jack Jr. did say you had one here."

"Of course," I managed. "Do have a nice afternoon." I watched Blake lead the way as the in-laws followed her down the front porch steps. I heard Eleanor say as she descended the steps, "I knew that girl wouldn't be ready. And I'll be amazed if she even has fresh towels out when we get back."

UGH!

"My Good God!" Vivi exploded when they had gotten in their car, you could freeze ice on that woman's ass!" She leaned over and kissed my cheek. "We got this honey. Don't worry." She smiled then turned and walked down the steps to her own car.

When the door finally closed and the house was empty I sat down on the steps that curved down onto the foyer. The old Mahogany bannister reached up to the top of the stairs. I sighed to myself. I had so much to do and such little time. But I knew one thing for sure. This house would be screaming

Christmas Wedding by dinnertime. Every room cleaned and decorated and I would at least have had a shower. Eleanor would be so impressed she would be speechless—exactly how I wanted her!

* * *

The ladies who I had hired to help me arrived and honey they were a sight for sore eyes. Five women spread out over the entire house and before I knew it the mansion sparkled like a new tiara. Fresh towels and sheets and every inch dusted and shined. And all in about four hours. I went through and was so proud of the entire inn. And the Frus Frus certainly didn't disappoint. With real greenery and garland hung from every fireplace mantel, wreathes placed over every bed, mistletoe hung in every-doorway and little amber lights twinkling from every single corner. The Fru Frus had so much help with them too. They made sure Christmas trees were placed in all the bedrooms and in each room downstairs. Coco and Jean-Pierre brought the hoped-for army of help and it took everyone—about twenty people worked for hours getting the place just perfect. As the cleaning crew moved from room to room, the decorating crew followed right behind. In six short hours the entire house was done, cleaned and fully decorated.

Jean-Pierre and Coco were the last ones out.

"Y'all seriously, just look at this place," I bubbled. "It's a winter wonderland, yet so cozy and old-fashioned. I swear I would think I was on the set of Downton Abby if I didn't know better."

"That's what you asked us for didn't you? A Downton Abby Christmas wedding with a touch of the Deep South," Coco reminded. "And honey, we do aim to please."

"Everything is just so elegant. Y'all have worked so hard and I can't thank you enough," I said filled with gratitude. I felt tears sting my eyes. I was truly living in my dreams at that moment. My house was so perfect. And I would be Mrs.

Jack Bennett in less than a week.

"And girl, seriously, if that woman has anything else to say about how ready we are or this stunning home, you let me know. She's gonna have to answer to us. I will snap her like a stick," Jean-Pierre promised, snapping his fingers, referring to Eleanor.

"Yes, girlfriend, like a stick. I get along with pompous like I get along with a rash," Coco added. "I'll have to scratch her eyes out."

"Now y'all, this is my new mother-in-law," I urged.

"You mean monster-in-law," Jean-Pierre smirked.

I reached up to hug them goodbye, thanking them again profusely, when all of a sudden a rogue squirrel came dashing inside.

"Oh my God, a rodent!" Coco screamed as he leapt up into Jean-Pierre's arms. "Please get me outta here! I just hate me a big ol' rat!"

"Get off me you idiot!" Jean-Pierre demanded. "That is no rat. That thing was a squirrel and it had a nut in its mouth."

"Lucky little rodent," Coco oozed as he dropped his long skinny leg to the floor to stand upright again.

"Please, in your dreams honey. Now move! We gotta catch this thing before we lose it!" Jean-Pierre ordered.

With that, we all took off as the squirrel scampered up the stairs, his nut in tow.

"I got it! I got it!" Shouted Jean-Pierre. I saw only his feet as he flew over the upstairs settee in the grand hallway and I heard a landing with a thud.

"Well, I thought I had it," he uttered. "Oww." He was moaning.

"Are you okay?" I asked running up the stairs. "Oh my word!" Jean-Pierre was lying on his back holding his knee to his chest. "Oh my God, honey. Can you get up?"

"There it is," he whispered. "Right there. Don't move." Jean-Pierre had his eyes rolled back to see the squirrel frozen—stunned in the middle of the hallway, the nut still in his mouth. His beady little eyes were twitching. I knew if I moved he would dash off. He was sitting just outside the room I had prepared for Jack's parents.

"Oh no, Please little squirrelly. Please. Shoo shoo, now. Go on to the back stairs," I begged. I was trying to sweet talk a rodent. It wasn't working. I knew if I ran for it he might go down the back staircase to the kitchen. But I had to do it just right. If I lost him, it would be a nightmare all weekend. I inched closer. Barely moving, I took a teensy little step. I was close. All I wanted to do was to get him away from the bedrooms.

Where all my guests would be.

Oh my Lord. Just the thought of that thing in the same room with any of them had my heart racing. One more tiny little step and I would be close enough to shoo him in the right direction. One more.

"Y'all seriously, you have got to know it's impossible to catch a rodent! Get up quick while you can Jean-Pierre and run while you can!" Coco landed on the top stair shouting and the squirrel took off holding onto that nut. I chased him, trying to run him in the direction of the staircase at the end of the hallway. All to no avail. That little rodent sped straight for the bedrooms down the hall when he suddenly stopped. He looked at me as if to say, *haha, gotcha*. And right into Eleanor's bedroom he went. Coco ran right behind me and shut the bedroom door, locking it inside.

"Well, now we have it cornered. At least know where it is, right honey?" Coco was grinning ear to ear like he had just locked up Santa Claus. Like okay now, off with your mask my bearded friend.

"No! No!" I shrieked. "Not in *her* room!"

"Oh God. Is this?"

"Yes! We have to get it out! They're gonna be back here soon," I begged. "Oh this is the worst!" I sank down into a chair along the hallway just outside the door to their bedroom. It was almost 5pm. I felt defeated.

"Heloooooo? Rhonda?"

I felt the blast of cold air from downstairs.

The wicked snow queen had arrived. And there was a nut bearing rodent just waiting to greet her.

Chapter Eight

I looked at Coco and Jean-Pierre. I had to think of something. Just then Coco spoke up.

"Send them away," he directed.

"Aren't you such a brilliant little thing?" Jean-Pierre said, sarcasm dripping from his well-chosen words. "They just got back you idiot! Where is she gonna send them?"

"No maybe I can—just a minute," I said with an idea in my head. I can tell them Jack loves mint ice cream and I didn't have a chance to go get it. I went to the top of the stairs and peered over the bannister.

"Eleanor, please calm down," Jack Sr. urged. "Take one of your Xanax. I'm sure it will help."

I was over-hearing their conversation.

"I don't know if I brought any," Eleanor snapped.

"Oh God Eleanor, I told you to bring the whole damn bottle. This week is gonna be hard enough." Jack Sr. was exasperated. He shuffled back into the parlor to find his Scotch, I was sure.

"Hey y'all," I yelled down to her. "I hate to send y'all

back out but could you run over to Piggly Wiggly and pick up Jack's favorite ice cream? He loves Mint Chocolate chip."

"I'm his mother dear. I know what he likes."

"Could you run out and grab some?" I asked again hoping and praying they would leave.

"I wish you had called before we got back," Eleanor sassed.

"I'm so sorry. I didn't have your cell number."

"Of course we'll go," Jack Sr. said popping his head out of the room just off the foyer.

"Can we pick up anything else?" He nicely asked. Obviously, Jack got his nature from his dad. Not his mother, Thank God.

"Nope thanks. See y'all in a bit."

I left the bannister and looked back at the Fru Frus. "Okay boys, what now?"

"We gonna catch us a rodent, that's what." Coco grinned. "I mean, he is." He shoved Jean-Pierre toward the bedroom door.

"Stop it!" Jean-Pierre limped. "I'm already hurt. I suggest you go get a shower and keep this door open. Maybe the little thing will grab his nut and make his way out by the time they get back."

"Just like I'm fixin' to do. Come on, nut, we need to get outta here."

He put his arm out for Jean-Pierre to hold and they began to make their way to the back staircase.

"Oh no, seriously? Y'all can't leave me like this. I mean come on—my in-laws have a squirrel in their room. Please? What am I gonna do?"

"Leave a trail of nuts and he will follow it right out the back door," Coco answered with a big grin.

"Is that what you do—follow all the nuts?" Jean-Pierre quipped.

"I follow you, don't I?"

Coco and Jean-Pierre walked past me as they headed toward the back stairs. I was alone in the house with no idea what to do. I decided to go get cleaned up and at least look presentable. I thought to leave the door to the bedroom closed. This way I knew where the little thing was hiding. I would have to tell Jack when he got home. I had just over an hour. I made my way to the master bath and closed the door.

* * *

Once I was ready I went downstairs. The house was immaculate and stunning. It was glittering with candles and white lights in every nook and cranny. We had pulled off a small miracle. Coco and Jean-Pierre had been magicians. The house cleaners made the whole place sparkle and all the evergreens woke up the house with the fragrance of a forest. I had put on my make-up to perfection and slipped on nice clothes for dinner. I even had on Blake's favorite Ruby Woo MAC lipstick. It was the perfect 1940s red. I was dressed in a black cashmere turtleneck and winter white wool dress pants. I had pulled my hair into a low side ponytail and tied a crimson ribbon around the hair tie. I splashed on a little Chloe perfume and waited. I went around and lit all the fireplaces, as well as all the candles on the mantels and hallway tables. I wanted to blow Eleanor away with how beautiful and perfect my home was and I knew I could. I actually was a bit surprised at how long Jack's parents had been out. I had fully expected them to return much earlier. I was in the kitchen with my red and white striped apron on when I heard the front door open.

"Oh I'm so glad y'all are back," I yelped from the kitchen. "Your rooms are ready, but I have dinner almost done so come keep me company in here. I have wine." I made my way to the front door.

"Sounds like I need to be in the kitchen?" Jack teased as he stood in the doorway. "Oh my! You have outdone yourself," he smiled as he gazed up the stairs.

"You're home a bit early," I smiled back.

"Who were you telling that their rooms are ready?"

"Your parents. Can you believe they came a day early?"

"They're *here*?"

" Yeah, but I sent them out about an hour ago to grab some ice cream for you while I finished up their rooms. They should be back any second."

"So we have a minute to ourselves? Mmmm, that sounds so good to me."

Jack began kissing me softly as he slid his hands around my waist to the small of my back. He smelled wonderful and looked even better, his end-of-the- day stubble brushing against my cheek as he slipped his mouth under the cowl of my turtleneck. I succumbed to him, kissing him back deeply, my hands slipping down around his perfect butt and giving him a playful squeeze.

Just then, "I cannot believe you, Eleanor. For God's sake go take a bath or something. And take that Xanax." His parents were in the same conversation as when they left. I heard the door slam shut.

"They're baaaaaack," I whispered into Jack's ear ala Poltergeist. "Have fun. I think I'll stay right here." I smiled and patted Jack on the rear end and sent him in to see his parents like a coach sending in a player. Only I forgot to tell Jack that his mother would have a little visitor bearing gifts in her room—my little friend the squirrel, and his nuts.

Chapter Nine

I woke early the next morning. The bright sunrise peeking through my windows had stirred me. Well, that and the bellowing of Eleanor. She needed extra towels. I was just so thankful Sir Mistletoe the squirrel hadn't caused her to fly into my room squealing. I let Jack sleep and got her the additional linens, saying a little prayer that our resident rodent had somehow found his way back to his tree—outside. He hadn't made an appearance all night so I had reason to be hopeful.

I wobbled to the kitchen, sleep still in my eyes. The early morning sky beckoning me to be part of it. Today it would all begin. By nightfall almost everyone I loved most in this world would be under one roof. My sisters were moving in for the week, along with their fiancés and their new in-laws. Annie would have Matt along with his dad and best friend. Abby would have Ben, his sister and his parents. My house would be filled with the bustle of preparations for the wedding, now only a few days away. I felt my soul swell with joy as I put the coffee and cider on the stove.

I sat quietly in the still peacefulness of that solemn quiet moment, alone in my kitchen and watched a cardinal in the Magnolia tree just outside the window over the banquette. His crimson feathers against the stark white sky drew me in. I knew what they always said about seeing a cardinal—the old wives tale. As the saying goes, it is like a hug from heaven—that someone you love that has passed away is watching over you. I felt my Granny Cartwright in that beautiful red bird. I knew she was right beside me, helping me be a gracious host, a joyful bride and a forgiving daughter to my troubled, somewhat crazy mother. Granny knew my mother tried but some of the nurturing genes were just missing from her DNA.

Mother Toots had tried to explain to me how it was that I had been the daughter of my uncle, my dad's brother, and not the daughter of the man who raised me as my father. She said, "You can't help who the heart loves. And I always loved Ron. He was the love of my life." I get it. But when you have made such a mess of your family, your responsibility as a parent to those children should come before your own happiness—they should come first. At least I think so. I know my sisters and me hadn't done a thing to deserve the hand Mother dealt us.

And now Mother Toots wants to be the fourth bride this weekend. My sisters and I all agreed. No. And that was final.

I drew in a deep breath and stared out at the December morning. Just then, the cardinal looked at me. He held his gaze. Was Granny Cartwright trying to tell me something? The little bird gave me peace, so I thought I was hearing her words, 'It'll all be okay chile', as she always said to me in her country accent. I loved that old lady maybe more than I ever loved anyone.

The doorbell rang and startled me causing me to jump up and scare the cardinal away. I shuffled to the front door and there stood my sisters, garment bags flung over their forearms, and suitcases standing upright next to them. They had both taken the rest of the week off from the radio station. Jack had planned to do his show today and then would be off the rest of the week.

"Oh y'all are a sight for sore eyes," I blurted as I led them inside. Get in here! It's freezing out there!"

"Oh my word, sweetie, this place looks like a wedding in Christmas town is fixin' to take place. I'm overwhelmed it's so stunning!" Annie amazed. "I couldn't love it anymore."

"Oh me too, honey! That staircase, I cannot even put into words what I'm thinking! I will be so proud to descend them straight into Ben's arms. It will be like a fantasy." Annie agreed.

"Oh I'm so glad y'all like it. The Frus Frus brought about twenty helpers and in a day they had it all done. They're gonna add a white runner to the steps the day of the wedding. But all those red velvet crimson bows, oh, I feel the same way—I was just overwhelmed when I saw it."

I led the girls to the kitchen and got them both a cup of coffee. We all scooted into the comfy banquette for some sister talk before Jack and his parents got up.

" I can't believe Jack's parents came early," Abby stated as she sipped her coffee. "What the hell?"

"Oh well, just wait till you meet the piece of work that is Eleanor Bennett," I announced. "She's in a league all her own."

"And I have a feeling nobody wants to play any kind a ball in that league anyway, right?" Annie amused.

"You got that right honey," I laughed and clanked my cup against hers. "And y'all, guess what else? She has a little visitor in her room and she doesn't even know it."

I leaned back against the banquette and drew in a slow satisfactory sip.

"Huh? Oh no, you aren't telling me the ghost of Granny is back are you? I know you thought you had ghosts in here when y'all were renovating," Abby asked full of doubt.

Abby never believed in anything like that. She was nothing like Annie who believed in pretty much everything, like the psychic, spirits—Annie was a romantic and so different from me and Abby. I did believe in signs though and I felt that cardinal had a message for me. But that's as far as I would take it. Not Annie. But I assured them I wasn't talking ghosts here.

"Oh no, y'all, I'm not talking about any looming spirits here. I'm talking about a real living breathing, rather unwanted, guest."

"Has Mother moved into their room? Oh my Lord, tell me Mother isn't here," Annie begged.

"No no, honey she isn't," I promised.

"Yet anyway," the sarcastic Abby droned prodding me to get on with it.

"No, I mean a rodent with a rogue nut in his mouth!"

"We have a rat! Oh no, I cannot do rats. I may have to go back home till you get it outta here." Annie jumped up.

"Sit back down, honey! It's a squirrel! And he's hiding in Jack's parent's room!" I smiled a little too wide I was sure.

"Oh my word, that is hilarious," Abby oozed. "If she's anything like you say, this ought to be wonderfully delicious!"

Just then Jack appeared in the doorway from the dining room. He was dressed for work in a navy cotton open-neck sweater with old-fashioned tan buttons, white-collared shirt peeking from his neck, and dark tan corduroy jeans. He had on tobacco brown expensive oxfords. He was a great dresser, sleek and clean-cut. And hot.

"G'mornin' ladies. Sounds like you three are already having too much fun. What's all the giggling?"

"Hey Jack, we're just telling bridal secrets, that's all," Annie offered.

"Morning Jack. We're almost there. Are you nervous?" Abby was more direct.

" Not in the least. Whatever goes on here this week doesn't matter. I mean I'm sure it will all be magical and memorable but all I care about is being her husband and getting on with the honeymoon."

I shook my head and smiled a knowing smile at him. "Spoken like a man."

"You know what I mean, baby. I just want the lazy days that are coming when it's just us." Jack had moved over to me as he spoke, then leaning in for a warm kiss he shot me a wink. I knew what he meant. And I felt just the same.

Jack left through the back door off the kitchen. "I'll grab something to eat at work. I think we're having food delivered there this morning. See you tonight, then it's wedding week, officially!" he skipped down the steps as he shut the door behind him—just as a fully dressed and coifed Eleanor stepped into the kitchen.

"Was that my Jack?" She dripped. "Oh, he didn't even say goodbye."

"Uhm, well, I'm sure he didn't even realize you were up. I know I didn't. It's still so early. I don't even have breakfast finished yet."

"Yes dear, I see and you aren't even presentable either."

"It is only 7am and as I understand it you weren't even due for arrival until later this afternoon. I'm Abby, Rhonda's sister." Abby interjected with sass.

"Nice to meet you. I came in early to help but well, she sent us away so we were here for no reason, as it turns out," Eleanor huffed.

"Rhonda, you are bound to be exhausted. I'm happy to get us some breakfast going while you go get ready. Everybody won't even be here till after lunch so why don't I just set out some rolls and jam?" Annie tried to help out as Eleanor began with her morning daggers.

"Rolls and jam? And you call this a B&B? Hrmpf, well I will get Jack Sr. and we'll just go out for breakfast. It looks like we might be a burden. I sure do hope you have it all together before Thursday night's rehearsal dinner, dear."

"Excuse me, but we are all about to become family and I for one think we all pitch in when it's the holidays. It's not like you're a paid guest here. I mean have you seen this place? It's like a magazine. Rhonda has outdone herself for all of us. While you're out, why don't *you* be a dear and get us all some breakfast?" Abby instructed.

"Well, I declare. I will go and be back when I get back. And not before. Please don't wait on *us* for breakfast. I am not in the habit of grab and go food. And by the way—you must talk to your maids—there was an acorn on my floor this morning and I almost tripped. Y'all have a good day."

Eleanor left the room with a dramatic pivot, her pointy little nose in the air. And just as we heard the front door close behind her, the three of us broke out in rolling laughter.

I grinned. "I just love me some squirrels."

Chapter Ten

I showed the girls to their old rooms—I gave them the same ones they had as children when we used to stay here while visiting Granny. The rooms were beautifully renovated and re-decorated but I made sure to keep out some childhood keepsakes and photographs. I knew they would be comfortable. I had divided the house, now filled with eleven bedrooms, all with their own bath and fireplace. We had to enlarge the upstairs corridors but it was worth it. The men and women would be separated and the parents and attendees would all have their own rooms. I had just enough space for everyone with one room left over, just in case.

"Oh Rhonda, this is gorgeous. I just love it!" Annie squealed as she twirled around in front of the fireplace in her room. Her warm smile told me all I needed to know. She was happy. She was a bride too.

I showed Abby to her room and she turned to me with a tear in her eyes, "I am in bridal heaven," she grinned.

I felt good. I left the girls to their privacy and headed into my bath to get ready. Just as I closed the door, my cell rang. I ran back into the bedroom and answered quickly before I got undressed.

"Honey, you aren't even gonna believe this but I think we may have a problem." It was Vivi.

"Oh God, what now?"

"That damn Myra-Jean. She went out to breakfast this morning with guess who?"

"Santa?"

"Nope. That would have been a win."

"I give," I said as I slipped off my robe.

"Your mother."

I dropped my robe and stood frozen. "What?" I yelped.

"Yep. I'm not even joking a little bit! Blake just called me and said she saw your mother with Myra-Jean up at T-Town café. They were in deep conversation. She said your mother looked upset. And guess what else?"

"Oh please, I can't take much more," I sighed.

"Blake said she saw someone else inside the restaurant, and honey you are certainly not gonna like this."

"Tell me damnit. I'm barely keeping it together here with glue and tape. I got a squirrel loose in my house and an old biddy trying to put me in my place every single second. I'm fixin' to throw me a hissy fit."

"Well, guess where that old biddy went to breakfast this morning?"

"Oh God, you gotta be kidding me! Jack's parents were there with mother and the psychic? Oh Vivi, please tell me Blake did not see them chatting—please?"

"Blake said she stayed hidden toward the back. She was getting a take-out order. She said she was trying to listen in and your mother sounded upset. Her loudness caught the attention of the Bennetts who recognized Myra-Jean from yesterday when she pulled her surprise appearance on your porch. Blake said she saw Eleanor wave to Miss Myra but said Eleanor didn't go over to her. She then heard Eleanor say to her husband something like wow, that woman sure didn't like what her future looks like, or something like that."

By this time I had sat down on the cold toilet seat top, completely naked and shaking. "Mother and Eleanor have never met. And now when they see each other, Eleanor and Jack Sr. will certainly remember her. Oh Vivi, I am so screwed."

"No no, I just wanted you to be aware so you can have no surprises when they do finally meet. You need to be ready and I can be there any time. Blake too. Just say when and we will both come right there."

"I love you for that too. But I am in this dirty bathwater all by myself."

"No! Now you listen to me. You are *never* alone. Never. Not as long as Blake and I are alive on this earth. You hear me?"

I heaved a breath into the phone. I heard her and she was such a comfort but I was Toot's daughter and my new in-laws were so pompous I was pretty certain it was going to be an explosion of some sort when they did finally meet. This little incident just put the cherry on top.

"Yes I hear you and I will most assuredly need y'all. The thing is I never know when Toots is gonna show up."

"Take control of it yourself, sugar. Invite her over tonight. We'll be there. That way you are in total control plus you have back-up. Us."

I knew she was right. I had to bite the bullet and do the introductions.

"Okay, let's plan on it. How about 8pm? I want to do it after supper. The last thing we need is for us all to sit down to dinner with both Toots and Eleanor. God help me, I will be taking Eleanor's Xanax myself."

"Alright. I'll call Blake. She had an all-day meeting out at Lake Tuscaloosa, some huge estate on the block and the kids are all fighting as usual when a rich ol' coot kicks the bucket. That was why she didn't call herself. I will text her and we'll be there. And don't worry. It's all gonna be fine. Keep your eye on the ball. You and Jack, married and gone by Saturday. That's all that matters. See you tonight."

I sat there on the toilet top staring at my freshly painted Christmas- red toes. This should be the very best week of my life. But here I was, as usual, trying to cover up the embarrassing behavior of my mother. It had been that way for as long as I could remember. I called Mother to invite her. She agreed, even sounded happy. She said she was bringing a guest. I was sure it was Uncle-Daddy Ron. God, my family. I shook my head and stepped into my hot steam shower and closed the door.

* * *

"Well hey y'all, come on in. So nice to meet you finally," I greeted as Bob and Shirley Flannigan, along with their daughter Britt as they walked inside. They were Ben's parents and his younger sister, Abby's soon to be in-laws. Britt was an equine veterinarian, one of the best in the south. This family owned one of the only racehorse farms in the entire state. As wealthy as Stardust In Dixie had made them at the Kentucky Derby this past spring, they were the most down to earth family, just salt of the earth type people—the polar opposite of my new in-laws and Eleanor Bennett.

"Hey y'all! Oh, I'm so glad y'all are finally here," Abby said entering the room and offering hugs to everyone. We had all gotten ready for the family arrivals. I had plenty of food and hors d'oeuvres set out along with coffee and tea and of course plenty of booze especially so Jack Sr. could survive being cooped up with his Mrs.

"Oh Rhonda, your Inn is so lovely. Thank you so much for having us all here for the next few days. It would be just what I would want, to all be together in the days leading up to the big wedding. You know, we almost had this day many years ago but anyway, I am just so glad we are all finally here," Shirley said as she walked around the beautifully decorated front hall. The twenty- foot tree stretched its branches upward to the ceiling above the banister. The entire tree was twinkling as the fire in the Christmasy parlor to the left of the front door danced in the distance.

Just then, Ben stepped through the front door, grabbing Abby up in his arms and kissing her. "You look amazing! Can you believe we're finally gonna do this?" He was gushing with joy, as he should be.

Annie had come downstairs looking for Matt and Mr. Brubaker. Matt's mother had died years ago and his dad was a reclusive man who lived deep in the woods of Connecticut now. Kind of a quiet mountain man. But so far they were not here yet. I tried to console Annie.

"Honey he'll be here. I'm sure of it. Just give it a few more minutes," I urged.

Everyone was hugging and chatting and wandering the downstairs with little white plates of food and crystal glasses of alcohol. Jack had arrived and scooped me into his arms for a kiss that made me forget all my angst, at least for a moment.

The house was warm and festive, filled with people we loved and all about to celebrate our first meal together. Then I saw Annie in the cove under the stairs on her cell. It was late afternoon and the winter sun was already setting. I was sure Matt was on his way.

"Okay but baby you have to get here at least in time for supper. Everyone is already here and mingling. Can't you reason with him?"

Oh no, it must be Matt's father. I hope he didn't change his mind. He was all Matt had. I was suddenly worried about Annie. I saw her hang up.

"Honey, is everything okay?"

"Matt said his dad will not leave the house. He made him put on a suit and his dad just wants to wear what he's comfortable in. I told him that was okay, just to please come on."

"Of course. I don't care what he wants to wear. He can come as he is. What does he want to wear?"

"A kilt."

"What?"

"You know, Scottish attire?"

"I know what a kilt is but why in hell does he feel the need to wear one?"

"Matt says it is the family tradition and he says his dad won't come until he can wear what he wants to. His kilt."

"Okay just tell him to put it on and get over here ASAP. I'm gonna have the Frus Frus here to help serve dinner in about an hour. I don't want them to miss it. I saw Annie go back to the little cove and make the call. She came out smiling.

"Oh thank you Rhonda, I knew you would understand."

"Honey, seriously what's one more crazy around here?" I laughed.

An hour later the Fru Frus came through the back door in the kitchen. Hands and arms filled with dishes, my own specialties warming in the oven. I directed them to put everything on the island and to make the plates and serve us from the Kitchen. Less confusion that way. It was already confusing enough. I said a prayer that it would all be okay as I re-entered the large dining hall. Just then the doorbell rang. I was sure I was fixin' to see an old Scot there with Matt.

Nope.

"Hey Darlin' I thought we'd come a little early, and looky who I brought with me?"

Mother Toots stood in my doorway nearly two hours early. Next to her was not the love of her life, Uncle Ron, Oh no, that would have been a relief. No. All done up in a large holiday caftan with matching headscarf stood five foot ten Miss Myra-Jean, the psychic. She was Mother's plus one.

Chapter Eleven

I had never hoped to see a man in a kilt as much as I did in that second. But alas, Mother was early and I knew the proverbial poo was fixin' to hit the fan.

"Oh sweetheart, so you're having a dinner party with the family and you didn't want me here for that? Why?" Mother asked dumbfounded.

I had to think quickly.

"I had wanted to speak with you privately and then have a special dessert and celebratory toast later with just you, Uncle Ron, and Jack's parents since y'all had never met. I didn't want that special moment to be with just everybody else and everyone just got here. I had wanted that time to be just us, but you're here now, so come on in. I'll get a place set for you both."

Miss Myra gave me a wicked grin and a nod as she swished by, her caftan taking up most of the space in the room. I knew there was nothing I could do. My sisters shot me a look. Blake and Vivi weren't coming until 8pm so I had to try to keep the explosion to a minimum with my sisters.

And there would be explosions, especially since Miss Myra had been warning me to stop the wedding and Mother had been pressuring us to let her be the fourth bride. Oh yes, it would be trouble. No doubt about it. I just had to control it.

The Fru Frus stuck their heads out when they heard the commotion in the dining hall. I motioned for two more places and everyone rearranged themselves to allow for enough space for Mother and Miss Myra. It was awkward and uncomfortable. But I knew that would only be the beginning. We all finally sat down at the dining table. The room was like a picture, with the fireplace roaring, the sun had set and the cozy atmosphere humming along, somehow I still felt the chill of the unexpected.

"Darling, could you please do the introductions? I do believe we're all fixin' to be related." Mother asked in a demanding, passive aggressive way. I got the message under the fake smile on her face.

"Oh, of course, please forgive me." I stood from my seat and did the formal introductions just as Eleanor's memory kicked in.

Great.

"Y'all know what? I saw you both today in some restaurant near campus. And honey, you looked mighty upset if I do say so," Eleanor said, her left eyebrow raised.

"Oh, uhm, well those were tears of joy," Mother stumbled. "Miss Myra-Jean has been my advisor for years and she says my daughters aren't the only brides to be."

Oh my word. Here we go. And before the first course is even served.

"Really? And, would you be that fourth bride?"

"Yes, can someone pass the potatoes?"

Sure Mother, like, I'm having brain surgery and could y'all pass the gravy? I felt my stomach twist. Jack slid his hand over mine under the table for support.

"I done told y'all this here wedding is doomed anyway," Myra-Jean chimed in. "I been trying to let y'all know you just gotta change this here date. I saw a real bad dark aura over it.

I need me some of that ham, please."

"Can someone tell us who this, uhm, interesting woman in the headdress is? I don't think we've formally met," Eleanor snidely remarked. "I mean she was here for a split second but no one really made an introduction."

"Oh," I jumped in—but was interrupted—by Mother of course.

"Let me, dear. This is Miss Myra-Jean Willows. She is my personal advisor and y'all can just call her Miss Myra."

"That is so interesting," Eleanor hissed. "Advisor? What kinds of things do you advise?"

"Oh you know, just stuff. Life stuff. Like the bad auras I see sometimes."

"I see. Not like investments. And just what is your education to be able to see these auras?"

"Well, I was blessed at birth. You know—born this way. I got a gift. And I use that."

"I see." Eleanor smiled painfully.

I saw Mother lean over and overheard her whisper to her gifted friend.

"Myra, remember when I told you to just be yourself— we may need to revise that a tad," she suggested with a tiny grin.

The twist in my stomach had become a full-blown knot. I glanced at Annie. Matt and his dad had not yet arrived. I had a bad feeling that things might actually get worse, though it would surely be tough to get much worse than they already were. I looked over and Abby was shaking her head to herself. Obviously as embarrassed as I was at the ridiculous conversation taking place over an otherwise elegant dinner. Bob and Shirley Flannigan just kept to themselves—and happily so, I was sure.

"Can y'all believe my daughter here didn't even invite us to this lovely dinner? I think she likes to hide me away," Mother gave a nervous laugh and shot me a nasty look.

I just smiled. "Why no mother, you misunderstood of

course. I had a special event planned for you and Jack's parents to meet since y'all had never met before. I had wanted it to be just us but this is fine. I'm happy you're here. You know that." Now the knot had turned to nausea. That was all I could do to get out that big lie. I felt Jack squeeze my hand.

"Well, *Toots* is it? I want to make sure I have your name correct," Eleanor went on.

"Yes, everyone calls me that."

"So, Toots, Jack did tell me you were engaged. I assume this is why you want to be a bride this weekend too. So where is the lucky groom?"

Oh please. I just fell down the rabbit hole.

I nearly swallowed my tongue. I had asked Jack to not reveal that the man I was raised to call Uncle Ron, was actually my biological father, due to Mother's affair with her own brother-in-law. It was too much for anyone to really understand and I knew that for Eleanor it would only give her an extra dose of venom to spew.

"Well, Rhonda did invite him to the formal thing she had planned for us later tonight but I called Miss Myra and she felt we ought to come early to make sure my daughters know just how important Miss Myra's visions are. I have never known her to be wrong and this is her advice, to cancel this wedding. Now. However, I do believe that dark aura gets a little lighter if I am also getting married, right Myra?" Mother was now embarrassing herself.

"Oh yes, significantly."

"Uh huh, but as you know mother, you and Ron deserve your own ceremony. We've discussed this." I felt myself speaking through my teeth.

Saved by the bell.

"I'll get it!" Annie jumped up and flung open the front door, the wreath nearly flung off into the green beans ten feet away.

"Matt!" She burst.

But it wasn't Matt. Where the hell was the man in the kilt? I actually was looking forward to him showing up. It would certainly give us something else to talk about. But no. Not Matt and his Scottish dad.

I looked at the man. Now there would be no secrets for me. No way to hide from the embarrassing truth.

The man standing at the door was Uncle Ron.

Chapter Twelve

I glanced at the door to the kitchen, Coco's head popped around the door, his eyebrows up, a shake of his sandy hair and he disappeared into the kitchen.

Disaster loomed.

Everyone stopped eating simultaneously. I saw Shirley lean into Ben and overheard her confused whispers. "Now whose daddy is this again? If he's Rhonda's dad and Abby's uncle, well, I don't think I get that?"

Sigh. I dabbed the corners of my mouth as if I weren't eavesdropping.

Of course, I was.

"Well speak of the devil! Get on in here, baby!" Mother stood up and motioned to Uncle Ron. "Y'all, I'd like to introduce my fiancé, Ron Cartwright.

He's Annie and Abby's uncle and my Rhonda's real daddy. This is my groom, y'all. Say hello sweetheart."

Wow. Mother was good. She got it all in— my entire lifetime of humiliated shame into one quick sentence. In front of my brand new in-laws and my entire wedding party.

"Huh?" Eleanor asked with her eyes squinted. She threw back her Chardonnay like it was Irish whiskey. "I don't think I understood. What are you saying?"

"Oh, I think I get it now," Shirley whispered to Ben who was smirking as he shoved a spoonful of potatoes into his mouth.

"What? Tell me," Bob uttered to his wife. "I don't get that at all."

"Hey everybody. Just call me Ron," my father said. Then he looked at me with pain in his eyes. Mother had obviously embarrassed him too. I looked back at him with as much understanding as I could muster. I felt badly—for all of us.

Silence. Then, in the nick of time, "Well hello everybody!! We finally

made it!" Matt Brubaker, Annie's man, and his funny father, all decked out in full Scottish dress, bounded inside. They were both wearing huge smiles and his dad actually had an accordion. He came into the dining hall dancing. They had no idea about the bomb Mother had just dropped on the dinner party.

Annie jumped up again and made a dash to the six foot five inch Matt, throwing her arms around his neck. He picked her up off the ground and spun her around in front of the soaring tree. Mr. Brubaker, Alistair, began dancing around them playing his accordion at full tilt.

I decided we all needed a break from this heavy cloud Mother seemed to have hovering over her wherever she landed. I led the way, getting up from my seat while still holding Jack's hand. As Matt's father played his music, Jack played along with me, spinning me and pulling me close. Laughter soon filled the large dining hall. The mantel sparkled with tiny amber lights, candles flickered on the white table cloth, as we all lost ourselves in the happy moment created by the eccentric Alistair Brubaker.

If only it had lasted a bit longer.

"I'm not too sure I fully understand," Eleanor says as Jack Sr. waltzed her over to me, her tiny boney butt bumping against mine. "Can you explain to me just how it is that this man is your daddy and that same man is also your sister's uncle? Jack, darling, did you know about this before you asked to be part of this family?"

Jack stopped dancing abruptly.

"Mother, I did not ask to be part of this family—I asked Rhonda to be part of me! *Me*! Frankly I am pretty amazed, even for you, that this is something you must keep pushing, keep questioning all these people, and keep trying to humiliate my bride in front of the whole family. This is actually not even any of your business. This information has no effect whatsoever on you. So mother, kindly, butt out!"

Everyone had stopped dancing. The music stopped.

Eleanor broke the embrace of her husband and stood perfectly still and straight, facing her son.

"Jackie! I have never heard you speak this way to me! Apologize to me this instant!"

"You have never attacked anyone I'm about to marry. And I will not apologize. Don't you see, Mother? You're humiliating her, putting her on the spot, making her feel insecure and insignificant. Is that what you're hoping to do? I sure hope not! Rhonda is going to be my wife, and I don't care who the hell is her father or her mother for that matter. I have loved her my whole life and all you ever wanted to do was keep me away from her. I just want you to stop. She is trying to play hostess to more than a houseful of people, some of them uninvited!" Jack was filled with emotion as he shot a disgusted look to Myra-Jean. "And remember, she is *also* a bride this week. Can you just back off for once and let her have her wedding week?"

"I'm just not sure I want you marrying into such a trashy family. I mean if your new mother-in-law couldn't decide whom she wanted to father all her children, maybe she should've have kept her dress on…and her legs together."

I was mortified. But what had he just said? Eleanor had always tried to keep us apart? What the hell did that mean? I furrowed my brow and glanced at Jack. He looked like he had said too much. Had he?

I scanned around the room. Everyone was standing frozen, staring. It was a deafening silence, everyone still and motionless. I looked at my sisters, my inexcusable loud-mouthed mother, and then at Jack. I wanted to disappear. I swallowed hard. I felt my mouth go dry. Tears began to sting my eyes. *Do not cry*, I told myself as the first tear slid down my hot red face. Mother began to speak but caught herself and stopped cold. The hurt and embarrassment on her face was palpable. Mother wanted to say something—defend herself. She shot a look to me and saw my tears. I couldn't take anymore. The shock of the moment was drowning me.

I began to run toward the cove under the stairs, but the sudden silence had summoned the Fru Frus from the kitchen. They had no idea what had just happened. Coco offered some much needed relief to the heavy moment. "Y'all ready for some dessert? We got it all ready to go. Three kinds of pie, crème brulee, red velvet cake—just name your poison." Coco felt the heavy atmosphere. " Oh, uhm, I'll just check back." His eyebrows popped up as he slid back into the kitchen. Now was not the time and I could see he knew that.

"Okay, listen everyone, why don't we all just sit back down and try to get to know each other," Ben's mom in all her sweetness suggested. "There is already so much tension and it's understandable. But hey, we're all fixin' to be family now so no need to attack each other. Have a seat okay?"

"Seriously? I can't sit at a table with a woman who has incestuous affairs. It turns my stomach." Eleanor was a royal bitch.

"Are you always such a pompous ass?" Ben's father, Bob Flannigan, said. He was a typically quiet, sweet man. But he obviously couldn't take Eleanor another minute. He blurted out what we all were thinking and sent the room into a tailspin!

"I beg your pardon!" Eleanor shot back as she stood right back up from her place at the table. "Jack! Aren't you going to say something?" Eleanor demanded of her husband.

"Okay," he began. "Yes, is your answer. *Yes*. She actually is always a pompous ass. Happy?"

He looked down and shoved in a spoonful of potatoes.

Everyone at the table burst out with laughter. Eleanor immediately pushed back from the table throwing her napkin down onto her plate. She made a fast pivot on her high heels and marched angrily upstairs.

"Oh please, forgive us, my family is a little taken aback with all the things going on. I'm sure Mother had one too many." My Jack was trying desperately to save face.

"Give it up, Jackie," his father said shaking his head. "It's who she is and we all need to just admit it. More whisky?" He took the glass bottle and filled Jack's glass then refilled his own.

Everyone at least had a grin and continued eating the last of the dinner. Eleanor had marched upstairs and I can promise you—not one person begged her not to go. As desserts were being served, I saw Mother lean over and whisper to Myra-Jean. They looked serious. I took one bite of red velvet cake and felt a twist in my stomach. I knew they were planning something—and that was never a good thing.

Chapter Thirteen

"Well, I for one know just what all this means," Mother stated like she had an announcement. Miss Myra nodded vehemently as she chewed her pecan pie. "You got that right, sister. Me too. I told you this waddin' gonna be good. I swear, I haven't been wrong about a wedding in decades. That and babies. I always know when someone's gonna have a baby too! But right now, it's this wedding—it's gonna be a fiasco. I know. I had visions."

"Then please, do tell," Abby finally popped. She was obviously becoming so exasperated. "Just what is it that you think all this means for God's sake?"

"You wanna tell her Toots? Or you want me to spill it?" Miss Myra quipped.

"I'll tell her. It's what we been tryin' to say all night. It was the whole reason I brought Miss Myra with me here tonight. We both been talkin' here but none of y'all is listening to a word we say."

She stopped to look at all of us. I glanced up and Eleanor was leaning against the bannister halfway up the staircase, listening intently. Suddenly everyone was quiet, hanging on the thick silence that hovered over the dining room. Miss Myra scanned the room with her steely turquoise eyes. She looked up at Mother who was now standing in front of her seat for the impending revelation. Miss Myra had an uneasy, piercing glare—as if telling Mother to go ahead. She had everyone's undivided attention.

"Y'all," Mother began, "what we've been trying to say is that the wedding isn't right—something's off. And Miss Myra has seen danger, I mean real danger. She has me scared to death for y'all's safety."

"Okay, Okay, wait a minute," Abby interrupted tossing her white cloth napkin down on her plate. "Are you saying that one of us is going to be hurt, like physically?"

"That's jes ezackly what I'm a sayin'," Miss Myra jumped in. "Y'all seriously gotta listen to me. Somebody here may be in a heap a trouble 'fore this here wedding is over."

"What are you seeing?" Annie asked with wide worried eyes.

"I see things all upset—I see someone crying and someone in an emergency situation, maybe even an ambulance."

"Right here at this house?" I popped with eyes bugging out of my head.

"Yep. Right here," she answered with a promise. "And somebody being carted out on a gurney. I'm a tellin' y'all. You gotta change the date. A different date and I see the all clear."

A sigh dragged out like a ragged breath over the stunned room full of soon-to-be brides and grooms.

"Rhonda, what are we gonna do?" Annie asked.

"Nothing," Abby snapped. "Absolutely nothing. I don't know about y'all but I surely am not planning the biggest most wonderful day of my life around a soothsayer. No offense Miss Myra, but this is my wedding day. And it's literally days away. I have never looked more forward to something or been more excited and so filled with joy over anything! The plans, the rehearsal, the families are all in place and we are all so filled with love and togetherness—it is a once-in-a-lifetime moment in all of our lives. It is in motion, Mother. Please back off trying to scare us. Hell, we have the bridesmaid's luncheon tomorrow. It's too late to make changes. Don't you agree, Rhonda?" Abby shot a look to me demanding I jump in and back her up.

I did—without any hesitation.

"Mother, seriously, this is happening. None of us are willing to make a last minute change with all due respect to Miss Myra. We have a million things left to do. The Fru Frus have already done so much preparation, I mean the food, the dresses, the decorations...the invitations are all out and RSVP'd. We cannot go backwards and run scared. Abby is right—this is the time of our lives so please don't try to throw a wet blanket on it for your own reasons." I shook my head with a glare at her.

I knew she was up to something because she wanted to be in the wedding. In fact, I was willing to bet if we allowed her to be in the wedding, Miss Myra probably wouldn't be seeing all this danger. I glanced to Annie and Abby. Annie looked nervous but resolute to stand with and me.

"No Changes, Mother. None. And that's final." I was resolute.

* * *

Later in the wee hours of the morning, as midnight had passed hours ago, everyone was safely tucked into their rooms. I couldn't sleep. I slipped out of bed and crept down the back staircase to the kitchen. The late night air—frosty, crisp and cold bathed my face as I stepped outside onto the back porch. I tightened my robe around me and shoved my hands deeper into my pockets. I drew in deeply and exhaled, watching my breath take form. The sky was a blanket of black velvet; a spray of glittering silver stars twinkled like sequins overhead. Another breath, exhale. A peace fell over me. I closed my eyes and could see Jack. He was a boy of fifteen, in the creek at Tannehill. His teenaged hands on me— the first time the hands of a boy had ever touched me. In that moment I could feel his warm lips on mine, in the cool waters, the summer breeze prickled my damp skin. My life changed—as quick as a kiss—and I never let him go. Jack moved into my heart that day.

I knew right then that no matter what Mother and Miss Myra were planning, scheming, I knew I would be Mrs. Jack Bennett in just a few days and that relaxed me. I tip-toed back upstairs to our bedroom and quietly clicked the door closed. The fireplace was down to embers and a flickering small flame, just enough to cast a glow over Jack's muscled toned back and arms. I slipped off my robe and slid in next to him, snuggling close, skin to skin. I could feel his warmth up against me. He stirred, but only for a second. The firelight cast an amber glow over the pale blush walls, my curtains puddled on the hardwood floors. Jack was facing me, my head lying on his perfect chest. He smelled delicious, felt delicious. I felt safe, so protected from the rest of the world.

Jack stirred again, his lips rested on my head, I felt him kiss me, then inhale deeply. "You smell good enough to eat," he whispered. I pushed my head up further into his neck, and kissed him softly. Jack's hands began to wander, his fingertips running along my naked body, he pulled me closer, moving his flesh over mine, kissing me, loving me, enjoying me. Jack gazed down at me underneath him, and grinned ever so slightly. The sweet heat of that moment was exactly why I loved him so, that and the moment earlier standing up for me to his mother. Jack was sexy, emotional, raw—without walls. His confidence was evident, enviable, everywhere he went. He was the most genuine man and I knew how lucky I was to have found one of the good ones. I felt special, one of a kind, desired and so safe now that I knew Jack was mine forever. He loved me. And I knew it every minute of the day.

I felt Jack's hands slide beneath my rear as he crawled on top of me and lift me up just enough so my backside rested on his thighs. His rugged face nuzzled down against my breasts, his lips tasting me as he traveled over my chest, and down my abdomen. I let him have the freedom he wanted with me, arching myself to meet his hips. I wrapped my bare legs around his buttocks and tightened them, pressing him toward me, inviting him to enter me. He came down on my breasts, his mouth, his sandy loose bangs brushing against my skin. His fingers tangled in my messy long tresses as he stroked my hair.

"I love you Rhonda. You're my life now, my everything. I want babies and a future and just us, our lives will be just us now. I want to grow into a family here with you."

I turned my face into the warm skin of his neck as he laid his body on me. "I love you too Jack. I want everything you want. Us. I love the sound of that. Us," I whispered onto his cheek. I felt his fingertips feathering down the fleshy sides of my breast as he began to thrust inside me. I wanted more. More of him. More of this and us...I loved him with every cell in me and I wanted to see him come apart above me. I wanted to know that we had done this together. I wanted to find our own beautiful rhythm. We made love in the dying firelight until the speckles of rising sun swirled and rose about us, a tempting pace, I was eager to match. I could feel Jack look for the pace where we both felt comfortable. I smiled at him. Jack looked into my eyes, his blue-gray eyes meeting mine were filled with softness. Without breaking eye contact, he began to move in and out maddeningly slowly. Then faster. His breath became ragged and heavy. I ran my hands through his thick golden brown hair. I watched him, loving me, and knew I was making him feel loved too. We were one. Jack and me. I began kissing his chest, moving up to his neck as he let his weight rest upon my breasts. I kissed him, as he sent tingles of heat shooting through me. I slid my palms down to the small of his back and pressed, in rhythm with him as he thrust deeper and faster, bathing him in pleasure until the moment we both shattered. Jack had opened his eyes and looked into mine just at the height of passion, and somehow, the emotions seeped through, tears filled my eyes—my husband.

Wrapped in each other's arms, sated and spent, Jack and I floated slowly back to reality but in a haze of passion, love, and heat. His hand drifting slowly over my back, I thought of the years that lay ahead with the man who I had loved and trusted since I was fourteen years old.

"I love you, Rhonda. And I know you love me. It's all that matters."

* * *

I knew Jack was right. I rested against his body in the twilight. Thoughts stirred in my head. I tried to fall asleep but I kept thinking, what if someone actually is in some sort of danger? I would never forgive myself. Miss Myra went as far to say she could see an ambulance in her vision. An ambulance? My heart jumped. I closed my eyes and drew in a deep breath. I focused on Jack's words, his body, his love for me—but still, sleep escaped me.

I had finally relaxed, just in the first seconds of dozing off into a much needed few minutes of rest, when I was startled by the buzzing of my cell on the bedside table. With sleepy eyes, I squinted at the number. I didn't recognize it. It wasn't in my phone contacts. I glanced down at the ominous text.

"Seriously need to listen to the warnings. I believe what Miss Myra is saying. Rearrange this wedding now or you'll be sorry."

I was suddenly wide awake.

Chapter Fourteen

Late that afternoon I met Blake and Vivi at Chicken Salad Chick. It was a popular place for us. One of our regular hangouts in Tuscaloosa. I had sent Blake a text last night cancelling the meeting I had planned with them at my house the night before. What good would it do—mother had shown up unannounced and with Myra-Jean the psychic. Even after the evening ended like it did, I still felt confident and sure in our decision to move ahead with our plans. My sisters and I were strong. And we knew our mother. No one would ever put it past her to be up to something to manipulate whatever she wanted. Even if that meant lying and conspiring with the town mystic.

But the haunting message on my phone that morning had thrown me. I was starting to worry. I had a big party planned at the mansion that night. It was a bridesmaid's party. All of the women, including the future mothers-in-law, would be there for my sisters and me. The Fru Frus were busy at the house making sure we had delicious finger foods and plenty of champagne. I had my dress steamed and ready, hanging in my bathroom. I felt very in control. The men would be at the University Club near campus having a party of their own. The consummate bachelor party complete with the most expensive cigars, Italian and French wines, and I didn't even want to know the rest. Oh I trusted my Jack with everything in me. And I knew with everyone's the father's there, the men would certainly behave. It was kind of a hoity toidy affair put on by Jack's parents. So it would mostly be a bunch of stuffy guys bragging about their great accomplishments. Huffle-puffing as I called it.

The girls on the other hand, had to deal with both Mother and Eleanor. Coco and Jean-Pierre knew this and promised a big surprise as a diversion. I didn't want to even think about that one either. No. On my mind in that very moment was one thing and one thing only—Could Miss Myra be right? Was someone going to leave my wedding on a stretcher?

Blake arrived first. She looked flushed, a little too pink. Like she was rushing. "Hey sweetie," I said patting the seat next to me. "Are you okay?"

"Yeah, just one of those days. It's my last day of work before I take some time off for Christmas and I'm just trying to get everything in before the day slips by. Plus I just can't wait till tonight." She patted my leg and she scooched in beside me. "So tell me, what the hell happened last night? I got your text but you never said what all happened."

I filled Blake in on all the details. But I could tell she was a little off. She seemed anxious. "Do you need me to go get us some ice teas?" I asked concerned.

"Oh, yes, do you mind honey? I just have so much on my mind, that's all."

I returned with three iced teas, anticipating Vivi's arrival to see Blake with tears in her eyes just as Vivi walked inside the restaurant.

"I knew something was bothering you. Sweetie-pie—its okay. We're right here," I assured.

"Honey—maybe you're just exhausted. You have been working so hard lately." Vivi stopped her thought, looking deeply at Blake. "Sugar, you look a mess. Tell us. We're right here for you. *No secrets, no burdens. We are never alone.* Remember our promise from our days as young Sassy Belles?" We all hooked each other's pinkies and bowed our heads together so our foreheads touched. We repeated the promise we had made to each other as children.

Blake and Vivi and I had started The Sassy Belles when we were all in the 8th grade. It was our little attempt at a youth-bathed answer to Steel Magnolias. We had been close all through grade school. We always took care of each other and had each other's backs. We created bylaws, and chants, and what we thought were spells. We were as close as friends could possibility be—but then, I had to move away. I lost touch with them over the years. But now that they had been back in my life for over two years, I felt like I had never left. They were my other sisters. And sometimes we were even closer than family.

Blake sat fidgeting and took a sip of her tea. Her lip was now quivering. Her hands began to shake as the ice cubes clanked in her glass.

"Blake, you're worryin' us. Come on honey. You can say anything."

Blake swallowed another sip then set the glass down. She smiled through falling tears as she began to speak. Vivi and I instinctively grabbed her hands.

"Y'all. I haven't even told Sonny. You know how I was throwing up last month all during Thanksgiving?"

"Yes, sweetheart—you had that terrible food poisoning. It was awful," Vivi recalled. Then she looked deeply at Blake. "Oh no, don't tell us something else is wrong!"

I felt tears well in my eyes. I loved this woman. What if...I couldn't even go there. "Please Blake, just tell us. You're okay right?"

"Well, I have been seeing a doctor." She drew in a deep breath and swallowed. "And I got the news today. Just now in fact. I just left the doctor's office."

"Damn it Blake! Tell us. I swear you're gonna give me a

heart attack," Vivi demanded.

"Y'all, I'm pregnant!" A burst of laughter filled the little restaurant.

"Oh my God! I was fixin' to die!" Vivi blurted. "Why in the world didn't you even tell us you suspected? I would have kept your secret! You know me!"

"Yes, honey I do, and that is exactly why I kept this all to myself until I knew for sure." Blake took a napkin and dabbed her cheeks. Happy tears. I was so relieved and thankful.

"You mean you didn't even trust *me*?" Vivi seemed a bit hurt.

"I knew you would tell Lewis. And then Lewis might congratulate Sonny and I surely didn't want my husband to find out I might be expecting, from someone other than me. So please y'all, I totally couldn't contain myself so do not tell a soul until you hear from me. I am planning to tell Sonny before the bridesmaid's party tonight. Okay?"

"Yes, yes, of course," I affirmed. "I'm just so so happy for you. Beau's gonna have him a baby brother or sister! When are you due?"

"Well, the doctor thinks I'm about 6 weeks or so along, so he gave me a due date of August 15th. I think I feel like it's a girl. But either way, I am just so happy. Sonny is going to be elated. He has been wanting another one ever since Beau got here!"

"Well you absolutely cannot even have champagne at my wedding," I reminded.

"Honey, Blake was never much of a drinker—the only time she was ever drunk was on a bottle of Nyquil and then she tried all night long to call me on her microwave," Vivi giggled. "She won't miss the alcohol one bit."

We all laughed and hugged each other. It was just the best news. Life goes on. I remembered what Jack had said when he made love to me that morning. He wants a family. Soon it would be my turn. I had a sudden thought—Jack had said that too. All that mattered was us.

But I knew I needed to show the girls my text from that morning. When we finished eating I presented my phone. Both girls sat, their mouths dropped open, heads shaking. "Who the hell is this from?" Vivi asked, an angry tone in her voice.

"That's the problem," I answered, "I have no idea. I was thinking Blake could help me trace it."

"Absolutely. Let's run back to my office. It shouldn't take but a second. I need to run home and get changed for the party. Plus I need to have a little chat with my hubs." She grinned as she slid out of her seat and we all followed her outside into the cold December afternoon.

* * *

We all followed each other to Blake's downtown law office and pulled in to the parking lot behind the old building. Blake ran into her office. Her legal assistant, Wanda Jo was there. She had worked for Blake since the day Blake and her ex-husband Harry had hung out their shingle. They divorced nearly three years ago and Harry won a seat in the senate and had moved to Washington. Blake ran the little firm by herself with a few interns from the law school. She sat down and ran the phone number from the text, then gasped.

"I totally cannot believe this. I thought we had at least one sane relative of yours left on this earth. But now I think I may be wrong."

"What?" I pushed. "Now you're scaring me. Tell me for heaven's sake. Who was it that sent me that warning this morning? Who?" I felt my mouth go dry like I had cotton in my cheeks. I licked my dry lips and swallowed with a gulp. "Do I need to sit down?"

"Maybe you'd better," Blake suggested.

I pulled up a chair and slowly sat down. "Who is it Blake? Mother? Miss Myra?"

"No sweetie. This phone is registered to your father, the one who is dead now. Donald M. Cartwright."

Chapter Fifteen

I was at home, standing in my own closet in my bedroom. I reached up to touch the winter white cashmere sweater I had planned to wear with my black taffeta circle skirt. I had the outfit in my arms when it hit me—a sudden breakdown. Too much down the garbage shoot as they say in therapy, and it all backed up and the tears fell fast, shoulders shaking. I sat down on the round velvet pale pink stool in my dressing closet. I felt the last two years bubble up inside me and without a warning I was too emotional to even get dressed. Abby and Annie heard me and they both came to see what had happened.

"Rhonda, are you okay? What happened sugar?" Annie popped her head in first.

"Rhonda, what's going on?" Abby pressed as she joined us.

"It's nothing," I managed. "I think it's all just too much."

"What? Are you having cold feet?" Annie asked.

"No! Not even a little bit. It's Mother. She just doesn't know when to quit."

Both of them stepped inside the closet, half dressed, in bras and underwear, and sat down on the carpeted floor. "What did she do now?" Abby asked as if she already knew.

"I picked up my cell phone from my antique dressing table and showed them the text.

"Who the hell is that from? I don't even recognize that area code," Abby was playing detective.

"I know. It's from the Gulf Coast," I informed. "It came from a phone belonging to Daddy."

"Your daddy or ours?" Abby jeered.

"Yours, you know, well, he was all of ours—the one that's dead now."

"What? You gotta be kidding me! Maybe Uncle Ron sent that," she reasoned. "Maybe he has Daddy's old phone. No! Wait," she added, "He doesn't have it in him. Plus he went down to the beach to check on his shrimp business for a couple of days. Did you find out where the call was made from?"

"Orange Beach. Right where Uncle Ron is right now," I muttered breaking down again.

"I know there has to be some explanation. I know it," Abby preached, squeezing my hand a little tighter.

"Of course there is, honey. I have known Uncle Ron my entire life," Annie soothed. "He was the fun one, the happy go lucky guy that played the piano while we all three danced around in the downstairs parlor. He would never be a part of Mother's scheming. Come on, get dressed. This is our night. Blake and Vivi and CarolAnn, and Britt will all be downstairs in just a few minutes. All here to celebrate us finding the loves of our lives."

"She's right sweetie, we gotta look like the diva brides we are," Abby agreed. "And you've already cried all your mascara off. Mother's not gonna do a thing to mess this up. I know for a fact that we put Daddy in the ground, and Uncle Ron is too sweet to do anything to you. We all have each other and we all have our sister Bffs. We are a force. Even for Toots. Now look at me—we gotta party to throw. It's showtime."

Abby never took anybody's crap. Especially Mother's. I knew they were right. But I was still uneasy. "I love you, Rhonda. We both do." Annie blew me a kiss as she and Abby closed my bedroom door. I washed my face completely and started over with my make-up. I knew I would need a fresh face for the evening, especially with Eleanor and Toots in the room. I wanted to be as confident as possible. When I was finally ready, I met my sisters in the upstairs hallway to make our grand entrance together.

"Y'all ready?" Annie smiled.

Abby and I both nodded as the three of us linked arms.

Coco and Jean-Pierre had been working away downstairs and answering the door. A party of women. It was going to be exciting. I felt much better now that I had my band of sisters. We made our way down the stairs like we owned the place. We did.

Just as we began to sashay down the stairs, big skirts with crinoline brushing against the curved bannister, feeling like the sassy princesses we were, the doorbell rang. Coco frolicked to the front door and flung it open. It was Mother Toots, all decked out in a white tea-length dress with a portrait collar ala, Elizabeth Taylor. The large swing skirt, flinging out, was bouncing with every movement. Her forced laughter screeched against the symphonic backdrop of Pachelbel's Canon in D major. I held myself together as thoughts began to cross my mind. It was my wedding week. My Bridesmaids party, and where was my mother? She was spending all of her time lobbying to be a bride herself—at the wedding of her three daughters. She never planned on giving up. I knew this now for certain watching her in that dress; work the crowd like it was her party.

I pursed my lips and inhaled as if to cleanse all the thoughts swirling in my head. I decided to play up all that confidence. I knew I was always a good little fibber. I had to be.

"Mother! You look beautiful! So glad you're here." I

leaned in for an air kiss but I felt her red lips on my cheek. My sisters greeted her, Abby checking the front porch afterwards as if looking for Miss Myra. Blake and Vivi arrived soon after, Blake just glowing. She had told Sonny and was on top of the world. Bonita came in with them, all nine months pregnant and still the most beautiful face in the room.

"Hey girl. Y'all all look just fabulous!" Bonita smiled. She was in a navy silk dress and cute navy patent flats. I swear she looked like she'd burst if she laughed too hard. But pregnancy sure looked good on her.

"Lord, y'all gonna have to keep me away from that cake tonight. My doctor said if I gain another pound, I may not make it to next week's due date. And I will not miss this here wedding for any man's money!" Bonita laughed, her low rolling sound filling the room with the cheer we needed. She worked with her husband Arthur, who was with the boys at the country club, at their BBQ joint but still worked with Sonny downtown at the police station. She was his number one investigator, tough and in charge. I admired her so much—smart and beautiful she was an example of one of the strongest Sassy Belles I knew. She would be part of the wedding reception, serving cake and punch at the bride's table. I had only recently met her when I moved back home to Tuscaloosa from Los Angeles, but it didn't take me long to love her like everybody else did.

Just then, Eleanor made her way down the stairs, along with Shirley Flannigan, Ben's sweet round mother. Shirley was dressed in crimson, one of the wedding colors. She looked adorable in her taffeta top and silk pants. Eleanor however was dressed to the nines, all in a cream silk suit from head to toe, her outfit matching her stiff old-fashioned hairdo—a French twist revealing dangling large pearl earrings. Her expensive designer high heels, Dolce and Gabana, were a cream patent leather, and she wore a throw over her shoulders. She was stunning with her blood red lips, which I hoped she would keep closed for once.

The party was well underway, everyone mingling and drinking champagne—well, all except Bonita and Blake, understandably. One more doorbell. Coco opened it to reveal two of my very favorite women—Blake's mother Kitty and her grandmother, Meridee. I had known both of these women my entire life. I had cried on their shoulders more than I had my own mother's. Usually it was my mother making me cry in the first place. I was so thrilled they both could make it! Kitty was in her signature hot pink skirt suit, and Meridee was a tiny little spitfire, all in Christmas red, at eighty-three years old, she was still smart and outspoken. She had been a role model for me when I was growing up. I spent so much time at her house with Blake and Vivi.

"Hey Miss Kitty, Miss Meridee," I smiled as I leaned in for a kiss on the cheek of each woman. "Oh I am so thrilled y'all could make it!" I reached my arms out toward them. "Come right on in and grab a glass of champagne." Coco immediately showed up with a tray of the bubbly liquid.

"At your service, ladies," he grinned.

"Oh darlin' your home looks like a magazine!" Kitty exclaimed.

"Oh it sure does! Oh sweetheart I am so very proud of you, Rhonda," Meridee commented. "You have done such a good thing here. You have to know that. Such important work, not only for your family but for Tuscaloosa."

"Oh, why thank y'all. It does feel so good to have the family home restored and looking her very best again," I agreed. I led them inside and to the parlor. All the women were walking around with drinks and little crimson plates of hors d'oeuvres. Candles were flickering on the mantels above roaring fires, as live greenery tied in silk crimson draped in ruffled edges on every surface. Conversation and laughter became melodic, a hum of joy in the background as everyone got caught up with each other's lives. Dim lighting floated overhead along with the fragrance of the 20-foot Noble fir that stood right in the crook of the curving staircase. The tree was covered in a thousand tiny colored lights, with satin crimson bows dotting the many branches. It was a festive perfect Christmassy scene.

I had been walking around greeting my guests, making sure everyone was comfortable when I saw Mother Toots talking to Kitty, Blake's mother. They were in the far corner of the parlor on the other side of the mahogany bar. It looked intense. Annie and her Bff, CarolAnn walked up to me and leaned in to whisper.

"Looks kinda intense dontcha think?" CarolAnn said. Annie was her spokesperson for her vintage dress business and she did regular fashion interviews on Annie's radio show. They were as close as sisters. She was Annie's only bridesmaid. The party was already so big with three of us getting married, we had all agreed to have one maid of honor, but I had two—because you know, Blake and Vivi come as one.

"Yes it looks like they are really into something," I smirked.

"But what? I mean with the faces they're making, I'm just hoping that Toots isn't trying to get Kitty on board to beg us to let her be the fourth bride," Annie joined in.

Annie was right. That thought was the first thing to cross my mind. Mother was out pleading her case, garnering support for her cause.

"Maybe you should go talk to her," Annie suggested.

"At least get closer to see if you can overhear anything," CarolAnn added.

I thought only for a split second. "Great idea CarolAnn. You go over near them and without Annie. They may not notice you if you're very careful. See what you can find out."

CarolAnn squirmed. "Oh do I have to? I don't want them to suspect me of eavesdropping."

"Yes, you have to," I demanded. "It's to help us make sure we don't have a wedding crasher named Toots. Now go!" I gave her a little push and a wink. "As a bridesmaid, you have to assist us, and this is where we need help right now." CarolAnn left the group and headed into the parlor.

Now if only Mother might suddenly get some sense about her and become the mother of the brides, instead of the bride. I saw Kitty becoming exasperated. Her hands perched on her ample hips; it sure looked like CarolAnn was walking straight into a firestorm.

Chapter Sixteen

CarolAnn looked back over her shoulder at us as she started toward Kitty and Toots.

"It's okay. You don't have to buzz around them too long," Annie prodded in a loud whisper. "I'll stay right here."

CarolAnn moved in closer to the women. The parlor was beautifully decorated with Christmas in every nook and cranny. The pale golden walls glowed with candlelight, and set the evergreen Christmas tree off beautifully. The room was dark, only candles and the large fireplace lit the room. I watched CarolAnn meander slowly to the bar, inching down toward the end near the ladies in the corner—they were still going full throttle, deep in conversation.

The history between Toots and Kitty was a thing of legend in Tuscaloosa. They had been friends, enemies, friends again and then just acquaintances. Kitty was everything Mother wanted to be. Kitty had many men fawning all over her for as long as I had known her. She had a way of casting spells on them. She was a flirt, and sassy and saucy all at the same time. Her rotund little figure never stood in her way. She knew she was beautiful and acted accordingly. It was confidence like I had never seen. She was genuinely funny and just loved people and social events. All that stuff came naturally to her. As did attracting men. She had been married five times. The last time was to the mayor of Tuscaloosa. They were still married now after three years. Kitty was hilarious and full of love and hot opinions, and always had her arms open to her ample bosom if you needed a good cry. I adored her. So much of Blake was made up of all the best parts of her mother.

Then there was Toots.

Toots wanted to be just like Kitty. She wanted all that male attention, she wanted to be the socialite. She wanted to be loved. But the thing was, Toots never knew how to give love completely, and totally unconditionally like Kitty did. Toots was awkward. Suspicious. Paranoid. Secretive. Untrusting. She wanted to appear to be something she wasn't. Easy-going. Popular. Genuine. The problem was, my mother, Toots Harper Cartwright, was none of these things, least of all genuine—which caused all of the other problems.

I was raised in a house full of secrets and bad behavior, and Toots was the unstable foundation. I watched my mother and my best friend's mother talk in the corner. It became all I could see. The rest of the house, the rest of the party, became a blur in my peripheral vision. It was like I was looking through a tunnel. Suddenly CarolAnn made a pivot and headed back my way at a clip. Annie had left my side to get more champagne at my request—I knew we were gonna need it.

"Well, anything?" I asked CarolAnn anxiously.

Annie arrived and handed out the much-needed bubbly alcohol.

"I was able to hear a little. Something about the wedding and Judge Harlon McCullough. Kitty did tell her to back her selfish ass off. I heard her say this was not her wedding day and it never would be and no she would not be helping her make it happen. Kitty said, '*I will most certainly not talk to*

Rhonda about it.'"

"Oh Annie, did you hear that?" I popped.

"Hear what?" Blake and Vivi joined us near the front hall tree.

"Oh Blake your mother is something else. I think she just put my mother in her place." Then I saw Blake smile and nod. It was clear what she had done—the reason she could promise me the other night at Vivi's that she would make sure Toots would not be a problem. She knew she planned to talk to her mother, Kitty. And anything Kitty said had great influence over Mother. It always had.

I was filling Blake and Vivi in on what CarolAnn overheard when I felt my cell buzz in my skirt pocket. Another text.

"Take this as a warning. This wedding will bring physical danger. Someone will be hurt. It could be bad."

It was from that same number. I felt like my mouth had turned to cotton. Suddenly it was too much. I needed some air. Blake and Vivi followed me through the kitchen to the back porch. The cold air slapped my flushed cheeks with a razor-like chill. I felt my throat go dry.

"Honey, let me see that," Vivi demanded grabbing my phone. She studied the text. "I'll just bet you that Miss Myra has something to do with this. Don'tcha think Blake?"

Vivi handed Blake the phone. "That could be. Except that the number is registered to Daddy Don and the origination of the call comes from down at Orange Beach. Someone would have to be running a router through a number at the Gulf. But still this actual phone number belongs to the girl's father."

I felt my eyes sting. "Why? Why is someone trying to ruin my wedding? I think this is even too low for Mother. And Uncle Ron, I would bet my life that sweet man isn't even aware of these calls."

"Look at me, Rhonda," Vivi said turning my shoulders toward her. "No body—absolutely nobody is gonna mess up this wedding, not even a little bit. You hear me? If I have to become an attack dog and stop people at the door I will. You have done enough to save this family, you have killed yourself saving what was once the haunted mansion here. You gave up your dreams in Los Angeles to come home and put the pieces back together and you grew up in the shadows of your mother's awful secrets, even learning that the man you called Uncle Ron was in fact your real daddy. Now I for one know you got happiness coming—Jack Bennet, is his name, and I swear on all that's holy to me, nothing is going to mess up this wedding. Now, dry your eyes, sugar. We got a party to get back to. And you are the guest of honor."

I leaned in and hugged Vivi tightly. She knew how to take over and make me feel secure. She was my Julia Sugarbaker. I glanced over to Blake, "Vivi's absolutely right," she confirmed with a sure smile. "I can run the search even tonight. We'll get to the bottom of it. It's just a scare tactic. I know it." Blake leaned in for a three-way hug between Vivi and herself and me. It was a moment. I knew it was one of those times I would be able to recall on any given day for the rest of my life—my girls and me, under a velvet December night sky, in the frosty cold air, standing there on my back porch in a group hug during my bridesmaid's party. I loved these two women more that I could ever express. And truth be told, they were part of the real reason I decided to leave LA and move home. I needed them. Yes, of course I needed Jack and was deeply in love with him, but it was my Sassy sisters waiting here for me, like I had never left, arms open and ready to take down anyone who crossed me. Oh they were still Belles in every way—soft and loving and oh so feminine, but believe you me, if you upset someone they loved, they could become a barracuda in 1.2 seconds flat. I was happy to be included in the category of someone they loved. Maybe I needed a new name for this style of Southern Belle—

Belle-accuda seemed perfect!

Just then, Bonita came bounding into the kitchen. "Ladies, I've been looking for you. I just got a message from

Tuscaloosa Police Department. Someone has called in a possible bomb outside the mansion. We're going on lock-down. Now!"

Chapter Seventeen

"A bomb? What the hell?" Vivi shouted, all three of us scrambling off the back porch.

"Yes, a bomb. It was spotted outside the mansion on the grounds but far enough from the house that they have asked us to stay put. I haven't been able to confirm where yet. I have alerted Sonny. He's the Chief of Police now so I'm sure he got the intelligence when I did. He's on his way here with the bomb squad. Right now we gotta get everyone to a place of safety. Is there a basement here, Rhonda?"

Bonita was all business.

"Yes, right over here next to the pantry. That door takes you downstairs," I said switching into high gear to help Bonita.

"Great, y'all help me get everybody down there. We need to be ready to stay there until we get the all clear." Bonita headed to the Grand Hallway and stood next to the big tree and shouted.

"Everybody listen up, she shouted gaining everyone's attention. "We all need to move slowly and without panic to the basement. Please follow Blake through the kitchen. She will lead you down the steps."

Everyone stopped cold.

"What's going on?" Coco questioned, panic in his voice.

"The basement? I cannot possibly go down there," Eleanor huffed. "My entire outfit is made of silk and Cashmere and I'll never get it clean after this. I'm going up to my room. Call me when whatever weird stuff y'all are fixin' to do down there is over." She began to priss up the steps when Vivi stopped her.

"I'm sorry. That is not an option. This house is under lock-down. There may be a bomb. Now please go to the basement. Police orders."

Eleanor suddenly looked like she had seen a ghost. Her mouth dropped open as she moved toward the kitchen steps. "Police orders?" Eleanor began to rant. "I need to know right now what all of this is about. I have my rights you know?"

Mother Toots and Miss Kitty jammed into the kitchen. "Yes, we all need to know what is going on. Are we in danger?" Toots tried to look calm, wide-eyed. I immediately suspected her, though I had no reason to at the moment.

Bonita stopped and turned to all the guests. "Okay everyone. A bomb threat was called in to this address. Apparently the call came in from an anonymous tip that a questionable package was spotted somewhere on the property. Right now I need all y'all to get downstairs and hunker down. I am in contact with the bomb squad, and Tuscaloosa PD, as well as Sonny Bartholomew, Chief of Police. Now please, slowly, without panic, everyone make your way down to the basement."

"Oh my God! I knew y'all were nothing but rednecks with newfound money. Y'all are trying to blow each other up. What a disaster! I'm gonna have a talk with my Jackie." Eleanor was in royal-bitch mode as she flung her cream-colored cape around her shoulders and pushed ahead of the other guests to make her way downstairs as if she were more important than anyone else.

"Did I hear Miss Bonita say bomb?" Coco asked. "Not the fashionista type, like she's the bomb, but *bomb*, as in the kind that blows us to smithereens?" Coco was verifying.

"Yes, honey, get on down to the basement," Blake ordered calmly.

"OH MY GOD!!! NO!!" Coco became hysterical and started screaming. "Oh Jean-Pierre, please, I'm not ready to die! I have to tell you I'm not ready. I haven't confessed to all my sins, and I just want you to know I love you and no matter what happens to us, I probably won't ever work with anyone else. Okay? I need you to be okay! Oh my Lord! We might die!! Jean-Pierre we might die!" Coco was losing it.

"Shut up you idiot! We're not gonna die. And no, you will not be working with anyone else, cause guess what? We're Not Gonna die!!" Jean-Pierre never liked the drama queen Coco could be in times of crisis.

All of us shuffled along, and when we were finally in the basement, Bonita closed the door to the upstairs and made her way down to join us. An ominous silence hovered over the cool cement room. It was like the times when Granny Cartwright would lock us girls down there until we could all get along. I felt like the adult as Toots, Kitty and Eleanor sat in opposite corners. Shirley sat with her daughter, Britt and Abby. They were most definitely already a family. I was filled with joy for Abby seeing them huddle together. Annie and CarolAnn were in another little nook by the extra food shelves we used to run the Inn. Blake and Vivi sat right by my side. Bonita took an old wingback at the foot of the steps, her emergency satellite cellphone in her hand.

I had to admit, all of us looked pretty scared.

"Well, I for one cannot even believe this is how your elegant little bridal party turned out. Figures. I mean from all we have found out in the last couple of days," Eleanor snarked.

"And just what do you mean by that?" Mother shot. She was sitting alone near an old refrigerator we kept for stock. Mother quickly stood up.

Here we go.

"You know, I guess you couldn't really help it. I mean that it took two men to have your children with. I guess you couldn't find a man to have sex with you more than once. I understand. It's just the incest thing I can't stomach." Eleanor had no threshold for how low she could go.

All of us sat dumbfounded in the little space. No one could even speak. Mother actually was so struck by the nastiness of the comment she had tears in her eyes. I swallowed hard and stood up. "That is my mother you are talking about. I know you are going to be my mother-in-law, and I can't tell you how sorry that makes me, but you are in *my* home, our *family* home, and there is no way on God's earth I will allow you to speak about my mother this way. In fact, if we are too low for you to associate with, you are certainly welcome to leave."

"Yes, and I will be happy to walk that lily white ass of yours right out of here myself," Vivi added.

"Nobody is going anywhere," Bonita interrupted. The bomb squad is walking around on the grounds right now. They have turned off the Internet so in case the explosives are connected to any cell service. No one can use their phones. Sonny is on the scene. Our men have been informed and are waiting in a safe zone. And please, can y'all be nice? This is like a bad episode of Housewives. I swear." Bonita shook her head and went back to watching her satellite phone.

"I'm not letting this one go. I think we need an apology," Annie suggested.

I shot Abby a look. She knew just what I was thinking. That old bathroom hadn't yet been renovated. We both remembered a bad childhood trick involving the toilet. I knew we were on the same page. I gave Abby the go-ahead nod. I would play along.

"Look we're all just tense," Shirley tried to soothe. "There's no need to be so mean though, Eleanor. We're all gonna be family soon."

"You know what, Shirley? I appreciate that you had one

racehorse win the Derby this year, but as they said in that movie, why don't you just go back to your double-wide and fry something."

"Ugh! Well I never." Shirley folded her arms over her big soft tummy.

"Hey, you don't talk like that to my mother you bitch!" Britt exploded.

Now Eleanor had insulted Abby's future mother-in-law who was as sweet as Melanie from Gone With The Wind. Britt, Shirley's daughter, was steaming.

Abby was steaming.

And we don't make Abby mad.

Eleanor was going down.

"I see you are really uncomfortable, Mrs. Bennett," Abby smiled acting like she cared. "Could you follow me so we can have a word in private?" Abby asked, standing to lead Eleanor to a dark part of the basement. Annie looked right into my eyes from across the room. She knew exactly what we were up to.

"Sure, if it will make you happy," Eleanor snapped.

"Just follow me," Abby smiled. "Oh can you excuse me? I might as well run right in here to the bathroom while I can. Why don't you go first?"

"Right," Eleanor agreed. "You never know how long this whole fiasco is gonna take." She made her way into the little bathroom and shut the door. I smiled as Abby shot me a look of satisfaction.

During the renovation, we chose not to do much to the basement. I was waiting until we had made our first fortune. Then I just never got around to it. And seriously, Eleanor was about to find out just how much work the basement bathroom still needed.

Suddenly, we all heard the flush.

Then we all heard the satisfying scream.

Then we all heard the rapid banging on the door, mixed with high-pitched screams again.

"Oh my God! This toilet is overflowing! Help me!! It

shot straight up my ass and now I can't get this door open!! My outfit!! The door is stuck! Someone please! Open this damn door! My new outfit is soaking wet and covered in brown shit. Open this God-damned door!"

I pulled the door just right, lifting it up instead of out as we had always done as children when we locked each other inside the *bad potty* as we called it back then. Eleanor came falling out as Abby opened it.

"Oh I'm so sorry honey," Abby dripped. "I couldn't hear a word you were saying with all that water spraying everywhere. I totally forgot. I can't believe that toilet's still broken. I thought you fixed that, Rhonda."

Abby was a genius.

"No, we decided to work on the basement later and no one ever uses it since we have so many nice ones on the other two floors."

Well! This just may be it. I can't take you people anymore." Eleanor huffed as she was walked back to her seat when she ran head first into a spider web.

"Aghh!" She screamed. "Someone get this freaking thing off me!" She was doing the spider-web dance flinging her arms and legs this way and that when her high heel snapped right off. She was batting away at the spider-web and limping along and covered in old poo water. And much to her dismay I was sure—we all burst out laughing.

"Y'all this isn't the least bit funny! Y'all are making me madder than an old wet hen! I swear I'm fixin' to throw a fit. Ani't no matter to me jest who's gonna see it either!"

What did she say? Hmm, I ran that back through my head. That sounded pretty country-fried to me. And we know Miss hoity toidy didn't talk that way. Or did she?

"May I ask, Miss Eleanor, where are you from originally?" Annie wondered.

"Okay fine. I'm from Alamo Mississippi. And that's the way my granny talked. When I get mad it just pops out."

"You mean that tiny town down near the gulf. Hell they didn't even get a grocery store down there till like 5 years ago," Shirley surmised with a grin. "Maybe *you* ort to teach *me* how to fry something, Miss Priss. You're no different than the rest of us—you're just one big ol' hick with money."

All that perfection. All that icy veneer—all melted. She was just a redneck in disguise.

Everyone sat together grinning back and forth. Until Coco spoke up.

"Y'all seriously, not that this hasn't been a little slice of heaven, but when the hell can we get out of here?"

Bonita got up and went around the basement. She found the upper windows and peeked out. "It looks like the bomb squad has the bag. They have it opened. Oh my word. You gotta be kidding me!" Suddenly she could see what was causing all the fuss.

"What? What is it?" I begged.

We all ran over to the windows. They were very high but we huddled together for the news.

"Well, that for sure, is no bomb. Coco you may have been right all along."

"What?" Coco raised his eyebrows.

That bomb is not bomb. It looks like fashion after all, like lingerie. Maybe someone dropped a gift off and a neighbor thought it could be a bomb, you know, see something, say something. But yep—I do declare that is some purty lacy jammies there Miss Rhonda."

"For God's sake!" Eleanor huffed. "That's our gift for Rhonda. That damn idiot I married dropped the present in the driveway." Eleanor shifted her gaze to our resident investigator. " Miss Bonita can you stay a while?" Eleanor was furious.

"Sure. Why?" Bonita asked Eleanor.

" You will need to investigate—I'm fixin' to commit a murder."

Chapter Eighteen

The next morning came with a strong winter storm. I could hear the cracking of tree limbs as the icy winds swirled outside. Slivers of frozen rain tapped against my windows. It had been such a long night—and certainly hadn't gone the way I had hoped. The bomb squad did a sweep of the rest of the property as a precaution. Someone had noticed the package left in the driveway and called it in. It was after midnight when the men were allowed to finally come home. They had been told to stay away until the all-clear had been given.

Jack had gotten up early and left to run last minute errands, pick up the tuxes, and check on the hotels to hold all the guests. It was so early but I couldn't sleep. Those text messages were on my mind but causing an even bigger shadow was Myra-Jean's prediction. Her dark vision of the wedding day. All those flashing red lights and ambulances were causing my heart to race. I wouldn't have wasted a single minute thinking about this but I remembered Blake and Vivi telling me about her predictions being pretty close to the craziness that had occurred during Vivi's wedding to Lewis.

My head was telling me that Miss Myra was in cahoots with Mother but my gut was pushing me to pay attention. I felt uneasy as my thoughts returned to those strange texts. Blake had said the phone was registered to Daddy. But I checked all the numbers I had for him and the number on the text didn't come up for him at all. The number didn't come up for Uncle Ron either. I was confused. But all I wanted to think about was my big day. It was so special for my sisters and me. While everyone in the house slept in, I was up thinking, and worrying. I knew Mother wasn't going to give it up and let go of her outlandish idea to show up as a bride on my wedding day instead of what I really needed her to be— mother of the bride.

I decided to be like our southern sister Scarlet, and tell myself I'll think about that tomorrow. I made my way tip-toeing past the guest rooms and down the back stairs to the kitchen. The bloated gray skies were a thick winter quilt hanging low and heavy. The sun would sleep all day and it was just as well. I had an entire menu of soups ready in the basement freezer. I whipped up some fresh croissants and put them in the oven and headed down to the basement to get some of the soups ready for all my guests. Putting together a scrumptious brunch would keep my mind busy and make me happy at the same time.

The basement storage area was in a bit of disarray from the night before—as my entire bridal party sat there forever, waiting for the bomb squad to discover my lingerie trousseau and spread it out all over my front lawn. At least it wasn't a real explosive. I couldn't help myself downstairs, I started to straighten things up, looking around and putting things away that had gotten displaced. I had become obsessed with being orderly, I was sure, because I was running a B&B now. Everything in its place all the time made life easier.

As I ran around cleaning up, I spotted something on a shelf near the old refrigerator. I didn't recognize the little device but I picked it up. It was someone's cell phone. I thought about it for only a second before I realized Mother and Kitty had been sitting in the same spot.

I knew it must be Kitty's since I knew what Mother's phone looked like. I ran upstairs and gave her a call, hoping she hadn't left for the morning yet.

"Hey Miss Kitty, I think I have your cell phone here. I found it in the basement this morning," I informed.

"Oh Darlin' I sure hope not, I have several showings today and my phone is you know—my life." She laughed as I heard her rummaging around for her cell.

"I've got buyers and Lord knows I need to close the deals, let me see," she kept chattering. "What does the one you have look like?"

"It's an older model, black..." She cut me off giggling,

"No, sweetie-pie, mine is hot pink, and all blinged out. You know, crystals and sparkles. If it don't shine, it ain't mine."

I laughed along with her. Kitty was one-of-a-kind. We hung up and I continued to think—surely this wasn't Mother's. I had certainly never seen it. Talking to Kitty also got me thinking about the very animated conversation she and Mother had during the party last night. CarolAnn had overheard Kitty's stance on the issue Mother had been pushing for weeks—"it's not your wedding day, it belongs to your daughters," she told her. I wish it would get through that thick brunette beehive of Mother's but she was stubborn if anything—to her core.

I stuck the phone in my pocket and scurried around to finish up preparing for a brunch, buffet style in the dining room. It would be easy and fast. Just what I needed. Two of the helpers I had hired for the week were due to show up at 8:30 to serve. Nedra and Daisy were priceless to me this week. They were both freshmen at the University of Alabama in hotel management. They would be serving and basically being my right *and* left hands. Nedra was short and chubby with dark eyes and long black hair. Daisy was tall and skinny with short a blonde bob. Both of them were bubbly and perfect for the week. I had given both a key so they could come and go to help me make sure we took care of everything, from changing sheets to cleaning bathrooms to purely taking care of the guests in every possible way.

I also had both of them on high alert for Sir Mistletoe the rogue squirrel, who was still missing. I knew for a fact though that he was still upstairs. His nut kept showing up in different places along the grand hallway. I just hoped he wasn't planning on being a wedding crasher—I could only take one and Mother had already claimed that spot.

I ran upstairs and spruced myself up to greet my guests when I ran into Abby in the hall. I showed her the phone.

"Did you look at it?" She pushed. "I mean, did you look up all the messages, and texts, and settings so we can know who it belongs to?"

"No, of course not," I blurted. "I thought it belonged to Kitty. Then I was getting the buffet prepped. I was just going to try to find the owner," I said innocently.

"Let me see that," Abby demanded as she snatched the phone from my hands. She went ahead of me and led me into my bedroom and shut the door. She began searching the device, even looking for the phone number assigned to it.

And then she clicked on the text messages.

Both of us sat in silence, on the side of my unmade bed, neither of us able to utter a single syllable. There they all were, the threatening text messages I had been receiving all week. Abby finally broke the silence.

"Okay so the phone is here, and Uncle Ron is driving back from the gulf as we speak. So he obviously isn't the one sending the messages, not that we ever really thought he was the culprit. And of course it certainly isn't Daddy warning you from heaven. It has to be mother. Although I have never seen her carry this phone. It's an older model. I think you need to confront Mother with it. If she denies everything, just give it to Blake to investigate."

"I just can't believe that Mother, as low as I have seen her go, could even do this. I mean this is ridiculous. I'm going to see her. Right now."

Abby stood up suddenly and turned to face me. "Look at me," she began. "No matter what she says, or how she begs, or how much she cries, do not, I repeat do not give into her and let her be in our wedding. She has been a pain and yes, I'm going to say it, a disappointment, for our entire lives and this day for all of us, marks the end of it. We have our own lives now and so does she. Please be strong, Rhonda. I will get Annie and we can all come if you need us to."

"No, no. I got this. Mother will feel like we are staging an intervention if we all show up unannounced. The whole thing has me infuriated anyway. You know we all are getting our dresses delivered this afternoon? The final fitting. We should be on top of the world, Abby but no, here we are dealing with Mother Toots again…I'm so freaking sick of it." I felt the sting of angry tears.

Abby sat back down beside me. "I know, we all lived with her erratic behavior and heaping pile of secrets, but it's ending. You got this, go end it—for all of us."

I hugged Abby then she stood and left the room, blowing me a kiss as she shut my door. I rushed to get ready, full make-up, and warm clothes to armor me as I headed into the icy December day.

The family was just padding around as I shut the front door to the Inn and headed straight to Mother's—

Chapter Nineteen

I drove the streets of Tuscaloosa slowly. An ice storm had been predicted and for once the weather forecasters had hit a bullseye. The city looked like a winter wonderland, frost and ice had formed on everything. Christmas lights cast a warm glow underneath the frozen crystals that clung to the decorations on everyone's lawn. We were just three days away from Christmas morning, and the city rush was coming to a quiet close. People Down South don't do ice, and snow is totally out of the question. So the streets were nearly empty as I made my way to Mother's. I passed the Christmas tree lot on the corner. Only a few stray trees were left under a hanging string of colored lights.

The city looked so beautiful all dressed in her holiday best. Christmastime was twinkling all over Tuscaloosa. The Bama Belle riverboat was all decked out, covered with big lights and garland. A large wreath hung from the deck as the red ribbons dripped in swag all along the rails. The Black Warrior River had a thin sheet of ice covering its surface, but just in places. Downtown was like a Dickens movie, wreaths and red bows hung from all the old-fashioned streetlights and the enormous city Christmas tree was all aglow on Government Plaza. It was the quintessential perfect little town and I was so happy in the depths my soul to be home. Finally home.

My tires spun in the ice a little as I turned onto Hackberry Lane, large tree branches hung leafless overhead, looking like they were guiding me through the scary forest in a Disney movie. I made my way out to Hargrove Road and turned right. Passing by places that took me back to my childhood growing up here, before we moved to Charleston, before Daddy left us, and before I ran off to Los Angeles to escape it all. It was a good beginning. Happy and solid, at least through my childhood eyes. But nothing is ever as it seems, so I learned when I uncovered the hidden, ugly family secrets that Mother was so good at hiding. That my uncle was in fact my biological father.

I rolled down my window and stuck my head out into the icy air. The frigid wind bit my face and I drew in a deep breath and exhaled. Today was a new beginning. I was turning the page. I was going from injured woman-child to adult lady, with my own life, my own husband. I had a new focus. My Inn, my husband and my future children. I felt strong, I felt powerful—and suddenly, before I knew it, I was in the driveway of my mother's house—and wonder-woman jumped out of my skin and ran away, waving her arms in surrender.

I sat still, gripping the wheel of my car. It was 10:30 am and I could see Mother moving around in her robe inside the over-decorated modest house she now shared with Uncle Ron. Her Christmas tree was in the far corner, the twinkling lights visible to the outside. Her lawn was covered in all kinds of decorations with things she had collected over the years. From a plastic manger scene to a blinking Rudolph, there was no design or thought, just all the things she had, all plugged in and—well, tacky. Mother had always wanted to be something she just wasn't. I actually felt sorry for her. I shook my head and knew what I had to do.

I glanced at myself in the rearview mirror and told myself this had been a long time coming. It was time and it had to be done. I got out and made my way up the icy sidewalk to her door, my nerves catching in my dry throat.

"Darling!" Mother greeted me, "To what do I owe this nice surprise?"

"Good morning, Mother," I leaned in to hug her. "I just wanted to drop by. I had found something in the basement this morning and I thought it might belong to you."

"Alrighty, well come on in. Can I get you some coffee? I'm fixin' to freshen up mine."

"Sure, just a little cream." I answered.

I took off my pale pink overcoat, laying it over the gold couch and had a seat in an aging crimson wingback chair near the fireplace. I rubbed my hands together both for warmth and to ease my nerves. Mother returned with the java and sat down across from me. She looked older than I had noticed before. Her make-up, her mask, off and revealing the real woman beneath the act. But still, her ocean-blue eyes were bright against her pale clear white skin. Her cheeks, flushed from the heat of the fire, lifted when she smiled at me. This was my mother. My flawed, messy, scheming, loving, well-meaning, manipulative, mother. And I suddenly realized how much I loved this chaotic person sitting in front of me.

But I knew I had to do what I came to do. I needed to confront her, so I took a deep breath and began. I swallowed hard and pulled the phone from my purse.

"Is this yours?" I asked as innocently as I could.

Mother's smile dropped. She reached for the device. "I think this was an old phone of Ron's," she answered trying to look confused. "I haven't seen this in years. How did you get ahold of it?"

"Mother," I huffed. "Please. It's time for all of this to end. I found it downstairs right where you were sitting last night. I have already been through all the text messages. I know you'll say you aren't aware, but I had been getting some pretty cryptic texts this week. And guess what—they were all coming from this phone. Besides this phone is actually registered to Daddy, is it not? Please, Mother. Be honest. For once." I was pushing her and she squirmed in her chair, shifting her weight and her eyes.

She looked away and sipped her coffee, swallowing with an exaggerated gulp. Mother stood up and walked over to the mantel and stood with her back to me facing the fire. "Okay," I heard her utter. "I found that phone in a cabinet recently and charged it up. It did belong to Don. But, I told Ron that just in case—we needed a house emergency phone. So I keep it charged and in a kitchen drawer just for that— emergencies."

"So I guess it was an emergency to threaten my wedding?"

"No, Rhonda, I did no such thing," Mother swore as she turned her face to me. "I don't know anything about those texts. I hate to tell you this but I did loan that phone to someone though. She had returned it to me just before your party last night."

Okay, here we go—mother's championship talent— deflecting blame. She was winding up for the kill. "Mother when are you going to stop? Don't you understand this is my wedding week?"

"Of course I do darling, but you have to believe me. I just got that phone back last night. I haven't had it all week. I swear it to you."

"Okay, so who had it? Do tell," I snarked, knowing I was most likely fixin' to hear a lie. It wouldn't be the first time.

"I can't stand to incriminate my friend but I had given the phone to Myra-Jean. Hers was broken and she needed one for the week so I loaned her that one. I saw her just before the party last night and she gave it back. I had it in my dress pocket and it must have slipped out during all the confusion with that bomb threat."

"So you are now actually saying that Miss Myra sent those texts to me? And if the phone was registered to Daddy, that's why all the messages looked like they were coming from the Gulf. That was where he lived after he left." I sat thinking for a minute, then, "Oh God, that is so original, Mother. I know you can do better." I stood up and walked over to her. She seemed so small and weak. But I had reached a breaking point with her lies.

"Mother, look at me," I demanded. "You are the one who wants to be the fourth bride, you are the one paying Miss Myra to be your spokesperson on this, bringing her to the family dinner the other night unannounced, and now this— this phone. You set her up to send those if in fact *she* even did—you! And you know it. When are you going to stop being so immature and manipulative? You try to control every single person and situation in all of our lives. For God's sake, this is my wedding week!" By now I was shaking and becoming visibly upset.

"Rhonda, you know I wouldn't want to ruin your wedding. I just want to be part of it," she muttered, her words shaking loose from her quivering lips.

"No, Mother, you don't want to be part of it—you want to be the *whole* IT—you want to be a bride. Do you realize you are robbing me and Abby and Annie? You are stealing a major part of this experience for us."

"Oh okay, right," Mother became defensive. "And just how, pray-tell am I stealing from your experience? Especially when I'm just trying to walk down the aisle with my daughters."

I huffed and shook my head. "How is it that you don't get this? We don't *want* you to be another sister! We need our mother. Can you possibly understand that? Because of your insistence to be a bride, we lose the *mother of the brides*. Don't you see that? It is a first wedding for all of us and we have no mother of the brides. No one will be there to calm our cold feet, to ease or nerves, to tell us we are the most beautiful they have ever been. Know why? Because our mother wants to get all of the attention as a bride! I need a *mother*. Do you understand me? I have *always* needed you to be my mother. We all, me and my sisters—we all need our mother. Can you be that?"

Mother looked at me, tears slid down her cheeks. She walked away to the front windows, fogged from the steam brewing inside the house. She stood motionless, now staring out over the tacky front yard. We hung in the heaviness of the moment. Silence. Finally she turned her gaze to me.

"I was trying," she said quietly. "I guess I never knew how. I'm sorry. I know I was never what the three of you needed but please, Rhonda, you have to know I was trying. I made a lot of mistakes. But I loved the three of you as much as any mother could. I just thought it would be fun to tie the knot together."

"No, to us we aren't just tying the knot. It's bigger than that. We are all so lucky to marry the loves of our lives and we need you to be with us as the mother of the brides. I can't and won't let you marry my uncle-daddy, the ugliest and most hidden family secret, on the same day that I promise to spend the rest of my life with Jack. No! It will absolutely never happen. Tell your attack dog, Miss Myra, she needs to back off. I'm done with this. As of right now, we are finished with this idea. You will not be a bride at my wedding. For once you will be what I need you to be—my mother. I have missed having that most of my life and it's high time you figured out what you need to do. Can you do it? Can you be our mother on the most important day of our lives?"

I waited for her response but she was quiet.

Nothing.

I got up from the chair and walked over to the large picture window and stood next to her. I was looking at a tired, sad woman. A woman who needed a do-over. A woman who knew her mistakes came at a great cost to all of us, especially me. I wanted her to speak—to yell back at me, hug me, anything but she just stood there—like her words had been stolen away.

I was determined to try one last thing. I grabbed her by the shoulders and gently looked into her face. "Mother, listen to me. I need you. I need my mother. I have always needed my mother and I always will. I love you and now we have a new chapter to try to get it right. Here is a chance for you to be the best version of yourself that you have ever been. You will get to see all of your daughters marry the man they love, and you alone will be the mother of the brides. That is so rare. And we need you immensely. Please, forget this whole thing and let's call Sweetie-Pie Jones and see what beautiful dress she can find off the rack for you—we only have a couple of days. Come on. It's what we need to do." I smiled softly at her, waiting for her response. She paused, then—

"I love you too, Rhonda, more than you will ever know. You are my first child, and the only child I have with the love of *my* life. You are my special daughter, and I have always been so very proud of you. All I ever wanted was to be close to you but it seemed the more I tried the further I pushed you away. I will proudly be the mother of the bride. I had no idea how important this was to you."

"Mother, it has always been so important for you to act like my mother. I need that, maybe now more than ever."

Okay, let's get the phone. I have Sweetie-Pie's number in my little book next to the sink."

Mother relaxed. So did I. Maybe I had gotten through, and maybe it would last long enough to get through the wedding. Mother shuffled to the kitchen to get the number.

"I'm glad you told me—besides, Ron and I are thinking of eloping anyway."

We both laughed and hugged each other. It was a long hug, healing and protective. Suddenly I pulled back.

"But Mother, what about Miss Myra?"

"I will talk to her. She never told me she sent those terrible text messages. And seriously, all that talk of seeing flashing lights and ambulances—I have no idea. I find it terribly hard to control Myra-Jean."

"Kindred spirits?" I mused.

"Very funny." Mother smirked as she walked back to her chair with the phone. She grabbed her cooling coffee and took a sip. Then she looked at me deeply.

"What?" I asked

"I'm so proud of the woman you have become. You are stronger and wiser than I ever was. I do love you so much."

"I love you too, Mother."

I just hoped I could trust her.

Chapter Twenty

The afternoon sped by at a clip. I was lost in my own head as the frigid icy day raced ahead of me. The morning I had spent with Mother had left me more nervous than confident—and emotionally drained. In my heart I was sure of how I felt about her, and even more sure that she really loved me and had done the best she knew how while I was growing up in the shadow of her secrets and lies. That was exactly what had me worried. At her core, I knew this was my mother—she could tell a fib and never blink. Commit a wrong, create a secret life, and for her—it was like drinking a glass of water. I felt uneasy even after all was said and done that morning.

As I raced around the house doing last minute chores, Jack came home. He felt the tension immediately.

"Hey beautiful," he said as he entered the bedroom where I was getting ready for the final fitting of my wedding dress.

"Hey baby," I said, my voice full of relief. Just the fact that he was home with me put me at ease right away. I felt myself relax. I met him at the bedroom door and snuggled into his chest.

"What's going on? I mean I know you're glad I'm home but I know that hug—tell me, baby, what is it? Was my mother at it again today?"

"No, it was *my* mother this time," I answered, kissing his cheek and pulling back to look at him. His eyes were soft and interested.

"Okay, tell me. She still isn't planning on crashing the wedding is she?"

"No, at least she says she's not. But I never really know for sure with her. She's a bit unpredictable."

Jack laughed. "Ha! That's like saying the Pope is a bit Catholic." Jack took off his shoes and settled into the overstuffed chair in the corner of the room. "Talk to me. I know the fitting is in an hour and I promise to be outta sight by then," he grinned as he put his feet up on the matching ottoman.

I filled him in on my entire morning. He listened with his full attention. When I finished he was quiet. I waited for his normally soothing response. But Jack looked full of thought and I could tell that everything I told him was making him think. I just hoped he wasn't feeling as uneasy as I had been.

"Say something," I said, "tell me what you're thinking."

"Look," he began, folding his arms over his lap. "I want you to really listen 'cause I've been saying the same thing for at least a month. No one person, not me, not you, not Uncle Ron, can control your mother. If you waste another minute of this week thinking about her and worrying and stressing, you're gonna have missed our best week—the best one yet, anyway—since next week's honeymoon will be even better. You have to let it go. I have had to let my worries about my own mother go—they are strong. fierce, flawed unpredictable women. In the end what can either of us do? But it does sound like she heard you. I know it took a lot out of you to confront her."

I moved closer to him and crawled onto his lap. I laid my

head on his shoulder and pressed my hand across his perfect abdomen, pulling him closer into my body. "You're right, I am so wound up with all the tiny details and my visit with my mother left me so tired. But I want so badly to count on her. Just for once – for her to be my mother, to show up and give me away to you—to be happy for me without think about what's in it for her." Jack interrupted.

"No, what you are wanting is for her to focus on you, to step out of the spotlight and let it shine on you. I understand that, baby. But whether that is within her wheelhouse, as they say, is beyond me. The thing you have to remember is that you told her what you needed to say—that you love her and need her to be your mother, just for a few days. Maybe it will sink in. But I want you to know and remember one thing—no matter who gives you away, no matter what happened on the way to you becoming officially mine—I am waiting for you at the end of the aisle…and that is all I am focusing on. Believe me, my mother is a piece of work too. But I am focused on you—and us. Okay?"

"Okay. I promise. I snuggled into his neck and exhaled. "Why are all these old ladies crazy?" I asked half in jest.

"I understand it happens to the best of them," Jack quipped. "All of y'all go a little nuts as you age, right?"

"Hush your mouth Mr. Bennett. Some of that cray cray may be fixin' to make a showing!" I jumped up and ran toward the closet as Jack chased after me, catching me and pinning me to the wall just outside the door. He kissed me hard and filled with passion, sliding his hands up my arms, and clasping my hands above my head. "I love you, so much baby—and life is gonna be great. You'll see."

I felt so energized and loved and free. Finally free of my insane past, my unpredictable childhood. I was starting my life with Jack. And he was right—it was all that mattered.

Just then I saw movement out of my right eye—a slip of a dark streak dashed from under the chair and slid across the hardwood floor, flinging itself under our bed. I let out a scream.

"Oh baby I knew you loved spontaneity but now? Isn't the dress supposed to be arriving any minute?"

"Jack! No, I mean yes but it's the squirrel—he's in here!"

"Well, no it's not a squirrel, it's me baby—you know, glad to see you..."

"Jack!! Listen to me!" I pulled away. "It's the squirrel. A real squirrel, like a rodent! He's under the bed. He came in the other day and we haven't been able to catch him."

"My God! Why didn't you tell me? I would have gotten him outta here."

"I saw him as your mother was arriving and she was already so critical of everything. I hoped he would find his own way out," I tried to explain.

"How did you think he was gonna get out? It's not like he's gonna open the door and say a fond farewell. And as far as I know, we don't have any holes in the walls up here for him to fling himself onto a tree. No! We've got to get Critter Control out here right away."

"No! Absolutely not!" I objected. "I will not have a van parked outside my wedding venue with the words "Critter Control" plastered down the side, the day before my wedding. All of the guests here will go nuts and want to stay somewhere else. I will not hear of it."

"Okay so just what *is* your plan here then? Just leave him be until we smell his tiny rotting corpse, possibly in one of the bedroom? I mean he has no food or water. He will die for sure."

"No, he brought his nut with him," I explained.

"What?" Jack popped.

"His nut. He had a nut with him and it continues to show up so I know he has something to eat." I was very positive.

Jack didn't buy it.

Just then, I heard the doorbell. It had to be Sugar Jones with the dresses. Nedra and Daisy were still working so one of them must have gotten the door—I heard Sugar downstairs and all the oooing and awwwing over the exquisite gowns began.

"Okay, Okay, I know when I'm no longer needed," Jack smirked. I'll go. I'll grab Ben and Matt and the other guys and we'll make sure the bar is properly stocked. But think about that squirrel. He may make a showing during the wedding and we sure wouldn't want that." He gave me a half smile as he slipped his shoes back on.

I smiled at him as Abby and Annie burst into my bedroom. "I think the dresses are here!" Annie said full of excitement.

"I love you, baby," Jack said kissing my cheek. "You ladies have fun." Jack grabbed his coat and made his way around my sisters, patting both of them on the shoulder as he passed into the grand hallway.

"Hey y'all," Shirley, Ben's mother said sticking her head in the door. "Y'all mind if we sit in. I heard the dresses have arrived." Britt was with her and I motioned for both of them to come join us. "Of course y'all can!" I confirmed happily. "In fact why don't we all go into the parlor down the hall? It's so big and I have plenty of seating," I suggested showing everyone the way to the large room. "I think we already have the room screens up so we can try on the new gowns."

Jack's mother stuck her head out of the bedroom, "May I join y'all?" She asked. It may have been the most civil she had been since she arrived.

"Of course, come on." I smiled at her. It was definitely time to unite. As we all made a parade down the long hallway I heard the doorbell again. My heart jumped for a split second—*oh please don't let it be Miss Myra with a new dark vision* I begged the angels. Then I heard the familiar laughter—Mother. I squinted and said a quick prayer that she was here to be Mother-of-the-bride, not bride. I hoped she hadn't brought her own dress and would be pushing to try hers on too.

"Abby, take everyone into the parlor and make sure they're all comfortable. I'll get Daisy to come check on y'all. Let me go see what Mother is up to," I directed.

"If she has her dress with her, show her back outside!" Abby had no patience with her at all.

I made my way back down the hallway and peered over the bannister. Mother was coming inside—empty handed. Whew.

"Hey Mother, come on upstairs, we're having our fitting up here in the parlor." I urged.

But then Mother turned around and took a garment bag from Nedra who was following close behind. She had obviously asked her to help her get it inside. It looked like she had her dress. *Oh Mother—when will you learn?* I thought. She took the bag from Nedra and began making her way up the curving staircase. I motioned for Daisy to lead the way.

"What do you have there?" I chirped as if to remind her, *haven't we already discussed this?* I shot her a look. She knew exactly what I meant.

"Oh Darling," she drooled. "It's a surprise—you're totally gonna love it!"

Chapter Twenty-One

I shook my head and turned to follow Daisy to the parlor. It was hopeless. Mother would always be Mother and I could either accept it or live in hell trying to change her. I decided to focus on doing just what Jack said, to think about us—me and Jack—finally being married and on our honeymoon in just a couple of days. I took a deep breath and exhaled away all the other thoughts and frustrations.

"Honey—can I just lay this on your bed?" Mother asked as we passed my bedroom.

"Sure. But we are doing our fitting down the hall. Sugar is already bringing the dresses in."

"Oh, I don't plan to try mine on with y'all. I'll just show it to you girls later okay?" Mother headed into my room and gently laid the pale gray garment bag across my bed. She turned and smiled at me. I noticed right away there was something different in her eyes, a warmth I hadn't seen in years. She even seemed calm. Do I trust this?

"Come on, darling," she said, slipping her hand around my back. "Let's go see that beautiful dress of yours."

What was happening? Whatever it was I was going with it. Mother was being motherly. The world might actually be ending. I smiled at her and we walked together to the parlor.

All the ladies were chatting and laughter filled the room. Daisy had lit the fireplace and the tree in the corner was a mist of amber lights and crimson velvet bows. The room was warm and festive. Mother and I took a seat near the crackling fire. I asked Daisy to bring up hot chocolate and coffee for everyone.

"Yes, ma'am this is just the best Christmas job I have ever had," she chirped. She asked each guest what they would like and took the orders, heading down the back staircase to the kitchen. Sugar grabbed the dress rack from the closet and rolled it out in front of us. Sugar was tall and willowy, with her long hair swept up on her head. She was in a beautiful black sweater and jeans and black suede booties. She was the epitome of style and every woman in town who planned to be a bride was on her waiting list for gowns. She was on her way to becoming famous and I knew her mother, the original wedding dress designer, Sweetie-Pie, was so proud.

As Sugar unzipped the garment bags and hung the dresses on the rack, all of us were stunned, mouths open as the ethereal dresses made of tulle, satin and lace, lined in white sequins, sparkled and glistened in the firelight. Each one was so different. So perfect for my sisters and me.

"Okay Annie, you're first," Sugar announced as she pulled Annie's vintage Cinderella creation from the rack. The huge skirt of tulle and white sequins was spectacular. The Basque bodice fell into a perfect V just below the waistline while the sweetheart neckline would frame Annie's face just perfectly. The back of the dress was a lace-up—a vintage detail Annie loved. Her train wasn't long to keep the princess-style look to perfection. A deep crimson velvet sash hung over the back, falling to the floor over the tulle and sequin short train. It was perfectly fitted to the fairytale that is our Annie's personality—vintage and creative.

"Oh my word, Sugar!! You have totally outdone

yourself!" Annie said jumping up to take the dress. "I have always dreamed of being a princess on my wedding day! I can't wait to try it on!" She took the dress and disappeared behind one of the privacy room dividers. Daisy had set up three, one for each of us.

"Alrighty, Abby, you're next," Sugar continued. She took a strapless form-fitting dress in satin from the rack. It was edged in the same deep crimson around the top of the bust-line and the bottom, drawing a rim around the entire train, all in white satin. Sugar had embellished the bottom of the front and the bust with a large pattern all in silver snowflake sequins. It was elegant, and so Abby. It would look perfect on her tall slim figure. She would be stunning.

"I can't even believe it," Abby said her voice choked with emotion. "It's a dream, Sugar. Thank you." I saw her glance over to Shirley, who was wiping away tears.

"Are you okay?" I asked Shirley, offering her a tissue from the side table.

"I sure am—this has been such a dream, for so long. That's all. I had just always hoped—Ben, he never stopped loving you and now for all of this—well I'm just so happy." Shirley took the tissue and dabbed her face. Abby stepped over to her and leaned down and kissed her head.

"I'm so happy too, Mom." Abby smiled through her own tears. I had never heard her call Ben's mother, 'mom'. It was really a moment none of us would ever forget.

Abby took her dress behind the partition just as Sugar announced my name. "And finally Rhonda, here you go." Sugar pulled out the most exquisite wedding dress I had ever seen. My own unique design. My gown was strapless and made of taffeta and lace, fitted to a dropped hip-hugging waistline, the lace dripping gently over the edge of my hips, meeting a deep crimson red taffeta ball-gown skirt with a long train in the back. A wide V was cut into the center of the train and filled with white silk ruffles flaring out from the dropped waist and down through the entire length of the train becoming larger as it reached the floor. Rows and rows of white silk ruffles. It was stunning and so different. I jumped up immediately reaching for it.

"Oh Sugar, I have never seen anything like this! It's just magnificent!" I hugged her and took the dress behind my partition. Britt came behind the screens and helped each of us get zipped in. We all waited until the others were ready. Then Britt gave the nod. We all stepped out from behind the screens at the same time. The light buzz of conversation in the room fell silent. The large oversized antique mirror over the fireplace shown our image—three brides, in perfect sync, in their own magical wedding gowns of white and crimson. We were frozen, staring up at ourselves. Mother Toots began to cry.

The usually catty Eleanor grabbed the box of tissues then spoke, her voice shaking. "Well, I am speechless. You three are the most beautiful brides I believe I have ever seen."

"My girls, my perfect beautiful daughters, this moment will be etched on my heart forever. I have never seen y'all more beautiful. I am just so proud—so very proud to be your mother."

I felt my eyes fill with tears of joy, as I looked at each of my sisters. They were breathtaking. I was standing between the two of them and I reached out my hands, clasping each of theirs into my own. My mother pulled out her phone and began snapping pictures, causing the others to all do the same. Everyone began posing and laughing and the phones were flashing, freezing us all in time. It was seriously the very best moment of the week so far.

I glanced over at Mother and our eyes met. She nodded and smiled and I knew what she was thinking—the pride in her eyes was evident. And I was proud of her too. She was so dignified and calm and attentive to my sisters and me. Maybe it had worked—that conversation I had with her that morning. Just maybe.

We all began to move back behind the screens to take off the divine gowns. Britt played the perfect lady-in-waiting taking the dresses all back to Sugar to hang them back up.

"I'll be here for the wedding and I will make sure all the dresses are ready and waiting. The attendant gowns will be delivered that morning. All four of them have already had them fitted so we are ready to go."

"Oh, y'all, they are just gorgeous," Britt added. "Floor to bust crimson with white sashes down the back. They are so perfect!"

"Aw, thanks girl! Y'all looked so stunning in them too," Sugar continued as she hung the dresses back on the rolling rack. "So I think we're all set. I'm just so happy y'all are so happy," Sugar laughed putting her hands on hips and surveying all of us. "This is gonna be a stunning, memorable wedding. I'll see y'all day after tomorrow—anybody need me y'all have my cell right?"

We all nodded and moved over to Sugar to give her hugs and thank her. Everyone stood and began to move out of the parlor when mother motioned for me to come over to her. "I still want to show you my surprise," she whispered. "Grab your sisters and come meet me in your bedroom, okay?"

Here we go. I agreed and grabbed my sisters and we slipped down the hall into my bedroom with mother and closed the door.

"Oh, I'm so proud of y'all," she bubbled. "You all looked so gorgeous."

"Thanks Mother, but what is this?" Annie asked, gesturing to the gray garment bag on the bed.

"Yeah, what is this?" Abby chimed in. "You don't have your wedding dress too, do you? I mean I thought Rhonda had talked to you about this."

"I did," I added. "And I thought we understood each other completely." I shot Mother a look, a pleading, hopeful look. She looked at me and smiled a small little grin. It actually made me nervous. Mother moved over to the bed and leaned down, unzipping the garment bag. Her body was blocking the view of what she had inside the gray plastic. We were standing behind her as she lifted the surprise from the bag and turned to show us what she had.

"Y'all like?" She grinned as she held up the perfect candlelight lace and crimson tea-length dress.

Not one of us could speak. Then Mother broke the silence.

"Aww, c'mon, y'all isn't it so pretty? —I'll be the most beautiful mother-of-the bride there. Y'all! Close your mouths—it's a mother-of-the-bride dress," she smirked. "Seriously!"

Chapter Twenty-Two

Over the next twenty-four hours, everything began to fall into place. The house was filled with good food, the bar was stocked, the gifts had arrived and my nerves were beginning to calm. It was Christmas Eve Eve—the day before the wedding and the bustle of activity in the Inn was putting me in the mood for both the holidays and the wedding. We were an hour away from the rehearsal dinner. The entire wedding party would be there, all the parents and the attendants and their spouses. The Fru Frus would be serving along with the girls and the house was filled with the aroma of apples and cinnamon, baking bread and stuffed turkey. We decided to have the full traditional spread. The wedding would be the center of attention tomorrow and the Fru Frus had planned a southern BBQ feast with Arthur. So tonight we were having the big bird with all the perfect fixin's, all set along the antique sideboards. The live greenery spread along every mantel filled the house with that perfect spicy pine aroma. My little Inn was bursting with Christmas spirit and everyone was scurrying around to get ready for the big dinner. The rehearsal had gone off so smoothly I could only hope the wedding would be just as easy.

I kept hearing the doorbell ring. Daisy and Nedra were welcoming guests and taking coats to the coat closet off the downstairs left parlor behind the bar. I heard CarolAnn arrive. Bonita and Arthur were already here too, as they were both family in every way. Mother and Uncle Ron, Vivi and Lewis, Blake and Sonny, Matt's father along with Matt's best friend Will Gables. We had never met him but he was slated to be CarolAnn's escort. Ben's family along with Britt's fiancé, another veterinarian from north Alabama named Brice Davis. We were all set as I finished my lipstick and headed downstairs to join everyone.

It looked like an old-fashioned Christmas card as I entered the busy atmosphere, laughter rolled though the rooms, and appetizers arrived on trays held by Coco and Jean-Pierre. Little crab cakes, stuffed sausage balls and cheese balls, steaming asparagus wrapped in bacon with Dijon spread on white doilies made it all very elegant as the champagne flowed.

"Darling, you have totally outdone yourself," Mother bragged as she leaned in for a kiss. "This is just spectacular!"

"Care for a sausage ball?" Coco popped in with his tray. "Don't mind if I do, even though I already have my little sausage ball right here," Mother said gesturing to Uncle Ron.

"Honey I hear ya. I swear I have the best tray. I could never keep my hands off the balls myself," Coco joked with a wink.

"Thanks honey," I said with my eyebrows up. I gave him a look to move along in case Mother wanted to have a longer chat about balls—which I wouldn't put past her.

Just then, Annie popped over, "Hey did you see CarolAnn and Will Gables?" She was excited. I looked up and could see CarolAnn in the parlor near the bar. Will was leaning into her and laughing. Then he kissed her cheek. He was tall and thin, muscular and lean with a mop of dark wavy hair. They looked adorable together.

"Oh my lord, he really likes her," I said to Annie.

"Oh I'm so happy for her. I have no idea where this guy lives but Matt has been friends with him for over twenty years," Annie explained. "They were best friends growing up. CarolAnn deserves to have someone good."

I could see how much Annie loved her best friend. Maybe it would really work out for all of us. Maybe this wedding would go off without a hitch. Maybe.

Jack snuck up behind me and snaked his arms around the small of my waist and snuggled his lips to the nape of my neck for a quick kiss. "Hey beautiful, can you believe how perfect this is? I mean look around. Everyone we love is all under one roof. I know I won't ever forget this. Don'tcha think?"

I turned to him, "I do! It is just perfect. I wish it could be like this every year."

"No reason it can't," he quipped. "The Inn is closed this time of year and we can always have Christmas right here. Everyone can come and we can re-create this every single year. We have plenty of room. It's so perfect."

Jack was right. We had this huge place and everyone could fit and all be together every year. The idea warmed my heart. I smiled as Jack kissed me slowly under the big tree. I had never felt so satisfied and fulfilled.

Jean-Pierre emerged from the kitchen with Coco by his side. They rang an antique dinner bell I had in the Inn to signal everyone to the long mahogany table. We had both leaves in to seat the large number of guests.

"I'd like to say a few words," Jack Sr. began as we all found our places around the table, the fireplace ablaze, the champagne flutes filled and bubbling. The room fell silent except for the crackling of the fire and the symphony of light Christmas carols playing over the speakers.

"I want to make a toast," he began. "To my Jackie, and his new beautiful bride, may you always be as happy and content as well... as well..." he stumbled " ...a pig in slop."

"What?" Eleanor burst. "A pig in slop? What the hell

kinda toast is that? Didn't you mean as happy as we are, Jack?"

"I thought that for a second but damn woman, I have to have a scotch in my hand nearly every minute to get through life with you," he laughed—but no one else did.

"Let me do the honors," Matt's dad interrupted. "I would like to make a toast to all the brides." His Scottish brogue heavier under the few glasses of alcohol he had obviously enjoyed. "You are lovelier than the rising sun, warmer than a midwinter's fire and more beautiful than the sea. Our men are all the luckier to have you. I miss my Marjory every day but seeing my Matt this happy, I know her hands are in this from her perch in the heavens."

"Here, here," everyone cheered taking a sip of champagne.

"My turn," Jack spoke up. " I just want to say thank you to everyone for sharing this very special time with all of us. And now, as I give my heart to my bride, Rhonda, know this—I have loved you my whole life, since my fifteen-year-old lips first touched yours in the creek at Tannehill. You have always had my heart—now we're just making it official. You make me better, Rhonda and I can't wait to see what all life brings us—it really won't matter because I already have what matters—you. That's all I'll ever need. I love you and thank you for finally saying yes."

Everyone cheered and the toasts continued around the table. Everyone wanted to speak. The mood was so uplifting as we all sat down to dinner. Coco, Jean-Pierre, Nedra and Daisy all worked the table, from the sweet potato pie to the buttery mashed potatoes, green bean casserole, squash casserole, black-eyed peas and so many different kinds of breads, all passed around the table amidst the laughter and talking.

The tall candles flickered and shortened as the lively evening wore on. We were nearly to the desserts when the doorbell rang. I had no idea who could even be outside, everyone we all knew was sitting around the big table in the dining room.

Nedra slipped over to the door and swung it open. The rush of cold air whipped into the warm space just as we all looked over and out into the darkness of the late December night—standing on my porch was Miss Myra-Jean in her pine green caftan, billowing in the winter winds. The look on her face was fearful.

I knew it had all been too good to be true.

"May I help you?" Nedra asked politely.

"I need to see Miss Rhonda, right now!" Myra-Jean was upset, almost hysterical. "Rhonda! I need to talk to you. I'm sorry to disrupt this here party you got going on but you need to know what I got to say."

"It's fine, Nedra, let her in out of the cold," I said getting up from my cozy spot in front of the fireplace. I wanted make sure Myra-Jean spoke to me in private. I tried to lead her to the bar but no such luck. She began blathering like an idiot the minute she stepped inside. Everyone in the dining room was silent, trying to hear her big news. Great. Just what I wanted.

"Oh Rhonda, you gotta listen to me. I was doing a reading for someone else and I swear I kept getting a vision. It was awful. You have to do something. This isn't funny anymore. It's real." Miss Myra was pacing now, all over the foyer. Jack got up and joined me as Blake and Vivi tried to keep the peace and calm in the dining room. It was to no avail.

"What are you talking about? What vision?" Jack snapped. "We're in the middle of our rehearsal dinner. I'm sorry but I think you need to go," Jack stated matter-of-factly. His hands on his hips, he had created a stance against Miss Myra going into the dining room.

"Y'all need to know. I am sure of what I saw. I know it's gonna happen and we can only do one thing to stop it. It's dark y'all. And I am so scared for y'all."

Mother got up and joined Jack and me in the foyer. "Myra, listen to me, Rhonda and I got this all worked out now so no need to keep trying to help me mmmkay? You can go on home—really everything's just fine."

"What did I hear?" Jack snapped. "You mean you and Miss Myra were in cahoots to try to stop this wedding? It's your daughters that are getting married!" Jack was getting fed up fast. "What is wrong with you?"

"Jack, I fixed all that. I promise that isn't what this is about. Mother is being good now." By the time we had reached this point, Abby and Annie, Matt and Ben had joined us all in the foyer.

"Y'all stop a minute and listen to me," Myra begged. "I have seen the event. I have seen the ambulance and first responders right here in this very spot. And I can tell y'all with all certainty—someone right here, right here in this house, is gonna spend tomorrow night in an ambulance."

Announcing the Weddings of

Miss Rhonda Harper Cartwright to Mr. Jack Bennett, Jr.

Miss Abigail Harper Cartwright to Mr. Benjamin Flannigan

Miss Annabelle Harper Cartwright to Mr. Matthew Brubaker

At the Southern Comforts Inn
Tuscaloosa, Alabama
December 24th at 7pm 2016

Chapter Twenty-Three

I had tossed and turned all night long, Miss Myra's words of warning playing over and over in my head. It had been a rather quiet day considering, or maybe it was just because I had chosen to stay upstairs doing my deep breathing. It was all so much and I needed to stay focused. I had hired one of my favorite make-up artists to come and get us all ready. All of the attendants, mothers, and brides had all been done to the nines. Hair, nails, and make-up all done to perfection had us poised and ready to take our places on the curved bannister. The sun had set and the clear December night sky was littered with a jillion stars on this perfect cloudless evening. I peered out my window as I sat alone in my room. Jack and the men had taken over the large upstairs parlor and I could hear their laughter coming from down the hall.

My sisters and I were all in our respective rooms awaiting the arrival of our maids of honor to help us get ready. It was a quiet moment in a sea of frenetic activity that was going on just outside my door. Memories of growing up here with Granny Cartwright filled my mind—and I so wished she was here to see what all I had done with the place, and see us all get married right here on this bannister, just as she had always hoped. Just then I heard a knock on my door.

"Y'all come in," I said expecting to see Blake and Vivi.

"May I come visit?" Uncle Ron murmured softly.

I was so surprised to see him. He looked wonderful, his white beard neatly trimmed to his sweet baby face. His black-tailed tux and crimson velvet bowtie and cummerbund looked just perfect on him.

"Of course," I answered with a big smile. "To what do I owe this delightful surprise?" I asked.

"I just wanted to see you—you know before you become someone else's." He took the footstool in front of the chair and pulled it up close to me. I was sitting in front of my antique dressing table in my baby pink silk robe.

"Just look at you," he smiled. "You are such a beautiful young woman. I need to tell you a few things, okay? Do I have time?"

"Yes, please. I have all the time you need."

"I needed to tell you Rhonda, how very proud I am of you and everything you have done for this crazy splintered family over the last two years. You know, my brother, the man you called Daddy nearly all your life, was such a special man. And the way he learned about me and your mom devastated him. He never knew how sorry I was, how sad I had been much of my life. He was raising my daughter as his own and no one knew—no one except your mom and me. The whole thing just created a cloud of immense sadness over everyone. There were no winners. Our family had been destroyed."

"Oh, Uncle Ron, really, you don't have to go into that right now. I understand." I wanted to know what he had to say but tears would surely make a mess of my make-up, plus I didn't need any sadness right that minute. But Uncle Ron insisted.

"No, no. Let me explain," he said. "I thought it was over

for all of us. You were way out in LA and I figured I would die before you ever knew I was your father. But then Don had the good sense to leave this dilapidated old place to you. And I knew he was a genius in his death. He was going to get you home to us once and for all. And just look at what you've done. My mother, your Granny Cartwright. is with us in spirit tonight and you have made her so happy. You've saved our family. You have put the pieces back together and we are all here tonight as a family. I have the lucky job of giving you all away in his place."

Ron stopped suddenly to wipe a stray tear. I got up and went to him, reaching my arms around his neck and pulling him close.

"I love you my daughter, can I call you that tonight?" He whispered.

"Oh I love you too, my dear father, and yes—we are father and daughter. And we will be forever. Thank you for telling me. You have always meant the world to me. I don't blame anyone for anything. We are what we are—one big messy family and I'm just fine with that. And like Mother has always said, the heart loves who it loves." I smiled. "Hey, you're the one who has to live with Mother for the rest of your life." I said trying to lighten the mood.

"She really is something else, you know?"

"Yes, that's for sure," I agreed.

"I love her. I always have and just know you were born out of all that love. It wasn't something cheap. I love that nut downstairs, and I know she loves her daughters. Now, let's go have us a wedding!" Uncle Ron stepped back and smiled at me. He turned and headed toward my door then gave me one last glance just as Blake and Vivi arrived in the hallway.

I was a little speechless as my two best friends came in and shut the door.

"What was that all about?" Vivi asked.

"Oh no, you've been crying," Blake blurted. "Are you okay?"

"Yeah, it was good. Really, really good," I said a feeling

of peace filling me. It felt like all the pieces had finally come together. "Come on, let's get me hitched."

You got it sister," Vivi nodded.

* * *

A half hour later I was in my stunning wedding gown. My long brown hair pulled into a loose bun at the nape of my neck and secured with a red velvet crimson bow. I stared at myself in the mirror. I wore a single strand of pearls at my neck, and one around my right wrist, and pearl and diamond earring dangled softly toward my bare shoulders. "Here I go," I said, my voice quivering. "How do I look?" I turned to my two oldest and best friends and saw tears in their eyes.

"You have never looked more beautiful," Blake assured.

"Oh honey, you are just like a picture, stunning. I'm just so happy for you," Vivi's voice shook with emotion.

Suddenly—

"Oh I feel like I'm gonna throw up," Blake blurted.

"Crap! Get to the bathroom now! She's been doing this all day. She has all day sickness—not morning sickness." Blake ran to the bathroom and Vivi followed her.

"Y'all, I'm gonna need you in like five minutes," I reminded.

"Oh she'll be fine," Vivi yelped from the toilet. "She's been doing this for the last two days. She has her nausea meds and some crackers in her purse. Don't worry."

They emerged from the bathroom, Blake fixing her lipstick as she walked, stopping to check herself in the mirror. I looked at her full of concern.

"I'm okay sweetie. I had this with Beau, too. I'll be fine."

"Speaking of Beau. He's gonna be the cutest ring bearer," I said.

"Well, that little detail has had a small upgrade," Blake divulged. "Jack really wanted—"

"Don't tell me—that dog of his? He asked y'all to let Bear be the ring bearer?" I asked hoping not.

"Well not all by himself. He wants Beau and the dog to do it together with Beau hanging onto the leash while Bear has the pillow strapped to his back."

"Oh good God, who came up with that,?" I asked.

"Jack. He thought it would be perfect," Blake answered. "It's okay, we practiced with Beau holding the leash. He's ready. I just worry he might decide to play his new favorite game."

"What's that?" I asked wincing for the answer.

"Beau loves this new game he made up where he's a bowling ball and the bowling pins are everything we own."

My stomach did a little twist. Beau was a tad over three. I hoped he could handle that big bulldog.

"How is Tallulah? Is she ready to be my flower-girl?" I asked with a grin.

Vivi's little redheaded mini-me was so adorable.

"Yep, she's more than ready," Vivi assured. "She is so proud of her fancy dress. It's all she's been talking about. She can't wait."

I drew in a deep breath and exhaled with a blow. My nerves were getting to me. All the small talk I was trying to create just wasn't working. Vivi could see me shaking.

"C'mon, lets get you out of this room," she offered reaching out to hold my hand. "It's really warm in here. All the men are already downstairs and waiting."

"Is the reception all set?" I asked nervously. The Fru Frus had set the entire dining hall with all the trimmings. The cakes, the red punch fountain for the kids—they had even moved all the furniture out of the large formal living room to create a place for our first dance. The house was ready—but I felt uneasy. Suddenly that vision that Miss Myra had of the flashing lights began to swim in my head. What if she was right? What if someone wound up in an ambulance? I shook my head as if to shake the thoughts out. It didn't work. I swallowed hard and pulled up the sides of my huge crimson taffeta skirt to make my way into the grand hallway. Suddenly, I saw my sisters. The stunning vision hit me so hard.

We were getting married—all three of us—together in our childhood home. Uncle Ron was right. I realized in that moment, I had done a good thing. Joy filled me like a rush of champagne as I walked over to them and held out my hands. "Y'all look amazing. Are we ready?"

"Oh, Rhonda, you look so beautiful. I'm more than ready. I'm beyond ready to be Mrs. Matthew Brubaker." Annie squeezed my hand.

"I am so happy y'all. I can't even think," Abby oozed. "I will finally be Mrs. Ben Flannigan. It has been such a long time coming. I'm ready."

Jean-Pierre came bounding up the steps and met us all in the hallway. He was organized and in charge.

"Okay y'all, I'll signal Coco so he can signal the little orchestra. You'll be walking down the steps and into the side parlor. They have set it up complete with an antique gazebo Jean-Pierre found. The orchestra is to the left near the large front windows. Judge Harlon McCullough will be waiting in the center of the gazebo to officiate. Just make your way down the steps as we rehearsed. Uncle Ron will meet you all at the bottom and escort you one at a time into the parlor. Annie you will be first followed by Abby, Rhonda you will be last. Okay here we go," Jean-Pierre finished with a clap. Judge McCullough had officiated every family wedding for decades. He was a family tradition.

Jean-Pierre signaled the four-piece orchestra and they began the wedding march.

"Okay you two, are you ready?" He said bending down to both Tallulah and Beau. Daisy held the bulldog on a short leash waiting for Beau to take the dog down the aisle. Daisy was waiting at the bottom of the steps with the dog as Jean-Pierre signaled Coco and he began to walk the children to the steps. Each of them made their way into the parlor, even Bear was good as he carried the pillow strapped to his back with the rings. So far so good. No one fell, though Tallulah kept stopping on her way down the aisle and asking if everyone liked her dress, chattering all the way to the alter, spreading crimson rose petals all the way as she walked. The babies were adorable. Amazing and well behaved for such intensity, too. I waited until they were both out of sight. Next our wedding party made their entrance, slow and staggered just as we had practiced. Then it was our turn. The orchestra began the wedding march and everyone stood.

All of us began the decent down to the bottom of the staircase to Uncle Ron. One at a time. He walked us all into the parlor to the waiting arms of our men. I was overcome with how perfect and beautiful the Fru Frus had decorated the house-turned-wedding-venue. Large white trees with white lights were in every corner. Crimson velvet ribbon fell from the top gently from the huge red bows that had been placed at the top of each tree. It was a crimson and white winter wonderland.

Jack looked like a dream, my prince charming in his black tux and tails, accented with crimson velvet. He stood waiting for me, staring at me just as Ben and Matt did, awaiting the arrival of their beautiful brides too. Lewis, Sonny, Ben's dad Alistair, and Matt's friend, Will, had all walked in ahead of us with our attendants. It was beautiful. My heart was overflowing. Our parents all lined the front row, Eleanor sat next to Jack Sr. Mother Toots and Uncle Ron took the seats on the aisle next to them. Once we were all under the large gazebo, Judge McCullough began the ceremony.

"Dearly beloved…"

We had all decided not to do individual vows because there would have been six of them. We all came to the conclusion that we would say our vows privately on our honeymoons. Just as Judge McCullough began the *Do you take this woman* part, Abby shot me a look. I looked back at her perplexed. We were in the middle of the ceremony after all. Then, movement from inside the tree in the grand foyer. A shuffling sound and an ornament fell from the top causing a crash. I shook my head at her—it happened to be right at the moment when Harlon asked, *Do you take this man*?

He glared at me and asked again, clearing his throat to help cover me. I was sure he thought I was just nervous. He was right! I was nervous that Sir Mistletoe was fixin' to make his appearance and crash this wedding. *Lord help us*, I prayed. *Please, not now*. Okay, I thought, maybe the big guy upstairs heard me. The rogue rodent settled down. I looked at Abby and she blew out a breath. I inhaled hoping no one saw what was happening. We had about a hundred guests and all the family and though the Inn was big—it was too small for the squirrel now hiding inside the main tree. All I could think of was *hurry it up Harlon; I got me a rodent to trap*. For God's sake let us just say I do already!

Then finally, "I now pronounce each of you, husband and wife. Gentlemen, you may kiss your bride."

All in sync, our men lifted our veils as we kissed our new husbands. Jack's lips were as soft as the day we were swimming in the Tannehill Creek all those summers ago. I looked into his beautiful blue-gray eyes.

"I love you, Mrs. Bennett," he whispered.

I tippy-toed up and kissed him right back. "I love you too, Mr. Bennett."

I looked over to my right to see Annie and her super tall prince charming Matt, really going at it—"Hey you two, you'll have a room soon enough." Annie's lipstick had smeared ever so slightly. I glanced to my left and Abby and Ben were still locked in their embrace, slow-kissing and stopping to gaze at each other, in another world all their own.

Everyone started to stand as the orchestra played us out into the foyer—right under the big tree. I dared to look up just as Sir Mistletoe stuck his head out from the garland. His beady black eyes met mine.

"Everyone! Let's get to the dance floor, I can already hear the music," I said trying to push everybody that way. But it wasn't working. I knew if I didn't get everyone out of the way, we all stood an equal chance of seeing the real wedding crasher from atop his perch in the Christmas tree.

Chapter Twenty-Four

Another ornament fell and splattered on the hardwood floor.

"This way y'all," Coco tried in vain to move the crowd away from the tree. Just then the tree began to shimmy and shake, all twenty feet of it. Sir Mistletoe was on the run, spooked by all the people. I could see his brown fur making his way from the top branches when suddenly he went for a huge dive right out of the tree, landing directly onto Eleanor's big white hairdo!

"Oh my God! Somebody help me! This rat's tryin' to kill me, hurry hurry Jack, help me!" She was running around screaming and hitting at her head. "Get this rat off me, I'm gonna have rabies. Somebody get me some Lysol." She was just like Lucy screaming at Snoopy after Snoopy licked her in A Charlie Brown Christmas.

"Look! Look! A kitty," Tallulah shouted as she began to chase the rodent.

"I want the kitty! I want the kitty!" Beau echoed as the two children ran around the back of the tree.

Sir Mistletoe jumped from Eleanor's nest of hair, and down onto the floor taking her huge hairpiece with him. The squirrel was squealing trying to free himself from the fake hair when Jean-Pierre quietly opened the front door just as our wedding crasher scampered down the front steps, Eleanor's wig still stuck to his front paw.

"And good riddance," Jean-Pierre said dusting his palms together.

"My hair, my dress, oh my lord, somebody get me some sort of spray!"

"What kind of spray do you need? Hair spray maybe? I'd say you need you some bug spray--those fake eyelashes now look like tarantulas sitting on your face," Jack Sr. laughed. "Pull it together honey, you look just fine! "Scotch anyone?" he headed on back into the large room all set for the reception. Eleanor ran to the downstairs bathroom just off the kitchen to pull herself together as we all began to head into the reception room. All the attendants were behind us as we formed the reception line to greet all of our guests. The orchestra moved into the large room, decorated in festive greenery, white trees with red velvet bows. The entire room shimmered with tiny lights and candles while two fireplaces lit the room with a deep warm glow. 'It Had to Be You' by Frank Sinatra began as all the brides took turns dancing, first with Uncle Ron, then the other dads. It was lovely, even if we did have a little visit from the rogue rat. As I passed by Abby, I gave her a look of satisfaction. When she got close enough, she whispered to me—"Okay so far so good. No one needs an ambulance."

I swallowed with a gulp. I had almost forgotten. I knew we had nearly made it with no real mishaps. Just a few more hours, I reminded myself. The lights were low and everyone looked so beautiful in the glow of the firelight and candles.

I suddenly heard the children laughing. They were loud and Bear started barking wildly.

"Oh no, what the hell?" I overheard Vivi shout as she dashed from behind me and ran for the edge of the dance floor.

"You gotta be kidding me! Sonny! I thought you were watching them!" Blake yelled, her voice filled with exasperation. Suddenly everyone was either laughing or yelling. The commotion took over and the music stopped abruptly. Everyone was staring in the direction of the red punch fountain—where both children had climbed inside and were splashing each other like it was a summer day. Bear was running back and forth jumping at the rim of the running red liquid when he pressed too hard and it sloshed over sides, covering the dance floor with the sticky red drink.

"Oh good God! Tallulah's dress!! Oh no!" Vivi rushed to her little girl and yanked her out of the fountain. She was stained from head to toe in red juice. Dark haired blue-eyed Beau had been all dressed in a baby tux, all white with white buckskin shoes. Now he was as red as a beet, from head to toe. The children couldn't stop giggling.

"Oh no, I'm so sorry," I shouted. "I thought they would love this fountain!"

"Oh honey, they did!" Vivi laughed. They absolutely did. Don't worry; I'll just take the clothes to Max over at University Cleaners. He can bleach all this I'm sure."

"Well, they still match the wedding colors," I pointed out—"Crimson and white."

It made her smile in the moment of chaos.

Vivi had a way of dealing with the insanity. Blake lightened up too, taking the children and handing them off to Daisy. "Give them a quick bath, and change them into their pajamas, then stick a movie in. I'm sure they'll be asleep in no time."

Blake and Vivi went to the kitchen and Coco returned with a mop. Before we knew it things were all cleaned up. I loved how they both just deal with things. Maybe you learn that when you have a baby, like osmosis, that skill just blossoms with your tummy. I was such a nervous person, I could only hope.

We all went back to the party, eating and visiting with

each other. The evening wore on and finally it was time for us. Our moment to just sit and enjoy the party. I sat down next to Jack. I felt his arm drape around my shoulder. "Are you ready, baby." He asked with a grin.

"What? Did I miss something?" I replied a bit surprised.

"No silly, it's time for our dance." Jack stood up and offered his hand like Prince Charming, bowing toward me with one arm behind his waist.

"May I have this dance, Madame?"

I grinned at him, "Absolutely, for the rest of my life."

The music began. "The Way You Look Tonight" began as Jack and I took the floor. Abby and Ben joined us, then Annie and Matt fell in. All three of us were living in such a magical moment. I felt like I had slipped inside a dream. I was in my own little snow-globe, a music box of everything I had ever wished for. I was in Jack's arms, and the ring was on my finger. My sister's and I had gotten married in our childhood home just the way we had always dreamed of it as children. I gazed up at Jack and he was staring at me, misty-eyed, and smiling.

"Pinch me," I whispered.

"I will as soon as I get you upstairs, Mrs. Bennett. I love saying that. I can't stop saying that."

"Never stop. Just never stop," I uttered.

The song was almost finished. We had almost made it through the entire ceremony and reception. No one had been hurt. No flashing lights. No accidents. That Myra-Jean was such a fake. A con artist. Granny Cartwright had always said that. The last few notes played out like the ending of a perfect movie. Jack spun me around, my huge crimson taffeta skirt encircling us as it billowed out around me. Jack took me for a dip, leaning down to kiss me just as I heard a blood-curdling scream.

"Oh my God!" I yelled as Jack jerked me up.

Everyone started screaming, looking for what was happening. Suddenly I spotted it. Bonita was lying in the floor, her water had broken and she was yelling for help.

"Vivi, grab the phone," I screeched. "Call 911! Bonita's in labor."

"Lord have mercy, we gonna have us a Christmas baby!" Arthur started to cry. It was less than an hour before midnight – Christmas morning.

"Oh my Lord, don't we need us some hot towels or something?" Coco panicked as he ran around in circles.

"Not unless you plan on delivering a baby right here by this wedding cake," Jean-Pierre snapped. "No! We gotta get us a doctor for her fast."

"We need an ambulance here to the Southern Comforts Inn," I heard Vivi say into the phone. "A lady's in labor here!"

I looked at Abby and Annie, both of them were nodding. That damn Myra-Jean. I couldn't even believe it. Jack looked at me and shook his head.

"Oh, Lordy help me, I am not able to do pain of any kind," Bonita groaned.

"Some damn body get my big ass some drugs!"

"Let me get to her," Matt pushed through. "I'm a paramedic. I can get her stable." He ripped off his tux jacket and knelt down beside an out of control Bonita. Matt rolled his jacket and put it under Bonita's head and began taking her pulse. Coco and Jean-Pierre arrived with cool towels and Matt grabbed them and wiped her face and forehead.

"God, is he not the sexiest thing you have ever seen?" Annie oozed.

Within minutes, first responders burst through the front door and made their way back to the reception. Before we knew it, Bonita was up and on the stretcher being hauled out to the ambulance, under a stream of flashing lights. We all followed her outside.

"What a way to end this night," Vivi said. "I guess Miss Myra was right."

All of us girls gathered on the porch watching the paramedics van pull away, the lights and sirens fading into the distance. Annie and Abby stood on either side of me,

Blake and Vivi just in front of us.

"It's unreal to me," I said to the girls.

"What?" Blake asked.

"That Miss Myra really has a gift. I just, well—I, I just never really believed she was doing anything but helping mother get her way. Now I see why she was sending me all those cryptic text messages. She was actually trying to warn me about what she saw." I surmised. "But still, I just cannot believe she really had a vision and saw all of this."

"Oh my darlings," Mother said from the corner of the porch. "I really can't believe what I'm hearing from you three."

"What do you mean?" Abby asked.

She made her way over to us and stood gazing deeply at each one of her daughters. She stopped her gaze directly on me. "You, my dear spent the better part of your childhood wishing on all those dandelions. And You," she continued looking at Annie, "laid in that front yard for an eternity looking for that elusive four-leafed clover, and You sweetheart," she said smiling at Abby, "couldn't take your eyes off of the night sky, wishing on every star you saw. All three of you have always believed in something. Remember? It's still there inside you. Don't let that cynical adult take away all that childhood wonder. The south is different form anyplace else on earth. We are so lucky here. It's a place where things happen, unexplainable things, where we love our ghosts and stories are passed down from generation to generation. Never forget what Granny Cartwright taught us all—there will *always* be Magic In Dixie."

Just then I caught a glance of Miss Myra-Jean off the side yard.

She looked over for a split second—as she disappeared into the Christmas night

THE END

A Southern Christmas Sampler

SWEET POTATO DUMPLINGS

8 yam patties cut in ½
2 (8) count cans of crescent rolls
1 cup water
1 cup sugar
1 stick butter
3/4 T of cornstarch 1 tsp. vanilla

Directions: Wrap crescent rolls around yam patties till no orange showing. Place in 9x13 baking dish

Bring water, sugar, butter to boil on stove and add cornstarch till mixed. Then add vanilla. Remove from heat and pour over crescent rolls.

Bake at 350 for 45-60 min. Sprinkle cinnamon/sugar over once removed from oven. Enjoy!!

Jill Lackey Sanford
Tuscaloosa, Alabama

PEPPERMINT BARK

One bag of white chocolate chips
A box of candy canes, I prefer the original red/white stripes.

Put the chips in a microwave safe bowl and melt. I find 30 second at a time works best.
Then take the plastic off the candy canes and put in a Ziploc bag. Close the bag and crush.
Add the crushed candy cane pieces to the melted chocolate and stir.
Pour mixture on a cookie sheet covered with wax paper and place in fridge to set up.

Once hardened break apart and eat.

Terri Walsh
Orange, California

GOULASH

Ingredients:
1/4 cup oil
3 lbs. beef (cut into 1" cubes)
1 lb. onion (3 cups chopped)
1 t paprika
1 1/2 t salt
1 t pepper
1 can (10.5 oz.) beef broth
3 t flour
1 cup sour cream
spatzle or noodles

Brown beef and sauté onions in pan. Add seasoning and 3/4 cup of broth. Simmer 2 hours. Add flour, remaining broth and simmer 15 minutes. Add a little juice from pan to sour cream and then add all the sour cream to pan. Serve over spatzle.

Veronica Dawson
Keller, Texas

SPATZLE

Ingredients:
3 1/2 Cups Flour
3 Eggs
1 Cup Water
1 T salt

Prepare a firm dough from the flour, eggs, water and salt. Beat until it comes easily away from the sides of the bowl. Press through a hand crack noodle maker. Drop noodles in boiling water until they float. Add butter to noodles if desired.

Veronica Dawson
Keller, Texas

DARK FRUITCAKE

1 cup nuts 2 cups sugar
1 cup blackberry preserves
I cup candied fruit
1 cup candied cherries
3 cups flour
1 cup raisins
1 cup buttermilk
1/2 cup cocoa
3/4 cup softened butter
1 teaspoon soda
1 teaspoon allspice
1 teaspoon cinnamon
1 teaspoon cloves
4 eggs
1 cup coconut or dates

Mix all together Cook at 275 or 300 degrees for 2 to 2 1/2 hours. Smells wonderful We had to make up the cooking temperature and time as my grandmother only gave my mom the ingredients She used dried fruit and cherries And of course homemade preserves.

From Kay F. Swindle
Your loyal Tuscaloosa fan

BREAKFAST CASSEROLE

2 cups shredded cheddar cheese
1 lb. cooked sausage
4 eggs
2 cups milk
½ t dry mustard
1 can cream of mushroom soup

DIRECTIONS: Grease 13x9 pan. Spread crutons on the bottom of pan. Add 1 cup of cheese over the crutons. Sprinkle half the sausage over the cheese.

Beat eggs with ½ cup of milk. Mix ½ cup milk with soup and dry mustard. Pour egg mixture over the first three layers. Then add another layer of cheese and then a layer of sausage. Over the top pour the soup mixture.

Cover tightly and refrigerate overnight.

Place in cold over set at 300 degrees and bake 1 hour uncovered. We have this every Christmas morning!

Veronica Dawson
Keller, Texas

DAWSON FAMILY CARAMELS

15 oz can sweetened condensed milk
1 box light brown sugar
1 cup light corn syrup
2 sticks of salted butter
1 t vanilla
Candy thermometer

DIRECTIONS:

Butter glass 13 x 9 really well.
Melt butter over medium heat, add brown sugar, then corn syrup. Stir constantly while over heat.
Gradually add milk, continue stirring.
Stir until mixture reaches 245 degrees.
Pour into pan.
Cool completely then cut into squares and wrap each square in wax paper. Do not cover pan while cooling.

This is a family tradition. We make several batches of these during the holidays and give them as gifts. Several friends ask for them every year!

Veronica Dawson
Keller, Texas

WHISKEY COOKIES

2 eggs
¾ c. sugar
2 c. flour
½ c. molasses
1 lb. pecans
1 box raisins (rolled in flour)
1 ½ Tbsp. water
1 ½ tsp. baking soda
1 ½ tsp. ground cloves
1 ½ tsp. cinnamon
1 ½ tsp. nutmeg
¼ c. whiskey

Mix all ingredients. (Roll raisins in flour before adding to mixture) Drop by teaspoon on greased cookie sheet. Bake at 350 degrees for 12 minutes.

Toni Henderson Smith
Gulfport, Mississippi

HOT APPLE CIDER

2 qts. (4 cups) of apple cider, if you can't find that, I use plain apple juice
1 1/2 qts. (3 cups) cranberry juice
1/2 cup brown sugar
1/2 tsp. salt
4 cinnamon sticks (I usually use about 6)
1/2 tsp. whole cloves (I usually use about 1 1/2 tsp.)

Mix all together in a big pot, come to a boil, turn off, put lid on pot and let it steep all day

Note: If company is coming, pour in a big crock pot to keep warm

Also Note: When it cools down, I usually pour it into the empty containers the juices were in, add a cinnamon stick and cloves into each container and put in fridge. Then when you want just 1 or 2 cups at a time, pour from the jugs, microwave.

Sonya Durrett
Tuscaloosa, Alabama
(Apologies, this is not from the Southern side of the family--it's from the Yankee side. But, it's practically the Crimson color of 'Bama. :)

CRANBERRY RELISH
(goes great with turkey, ham or pork)

1 bag of cranberries, chopped (closest thing they have to a pound--they screw up the recipes when they downsize)
2 cups of apples, chopped
1 cup English walnuts, chopped
2 cups granulated sugar
1 1/2 cup boiling water
2 small box or 1 large box of cherry Jell-O

Combine sugar, water, Jell-O and dissolve. Add nuts, cranberries, and apples--stir. Put into your favorite serving dish--mine is a real pretty, glass antique footed bowl. Put in refrigerator until firm--several hours. Don't forget to put plastic wrap over the top to keep it safe.

Denise Holcomb

SWEET POTATO CASSEROLE

6 or 8 sweet potatoes, peeled and cut into 1-inch cubes
3/4 cup packed brown sugar
1/4 cup butter, softened
1 1/2 teaspoons salt
1/2 teaspoon vanilla extract
1/2 cup finely chopped pecans, divided
Cooking spray
2 cups miniature marshmallows

Preparation

Preheat oven to 375°.

Place the sweet potatoes in a large pot, and cover with cold water. Bring to a boil. Reduce heat, and simmer for 15 minutes or until very tender. Drain; cool slightly.

Place potatoes in a large bowl. Add next 4 ingredients. Mash sweet potato mixture with a potato masher. Fold in 1/4 cup pecans. Scrape potato mixture into an even layer in an 11 x 7-inch baking dish coated with cooking spray. Sprinkle with remaining 1/4 cup pecans; top with marshmallows. Bake at 375° for 25 minutes or until golden.

Connie Hunnicutt Stringer
Tuscaloosa, Alabama

HATTIE'S MULTI USE PIE FILLING

(We use it every holiday!)
1 cup sugar
1 cup milk
2 eggs separated
3 T. Flour mixed in very warm water
Pinch of salt
1t. Vanilla
Reserve egg whites for meringue

Mix all ingredients together and bring to a boil. Cook until thick while stirring often.

For Chocolate Pie Filling add 3 T. Cocoa powder mixed in a little warm water and stir.

For Coconut Pie Filling add 1 of coconut and stir.

For Banana pudding pour over layers of vanilla wafers and bananas.

For Meringue beat the egg whites till stiff. Stir in 3T of sugar and beat again until stiff and white. Spread over pies or pudding and bake until golden brown.

This recipe uses 9 inch pie shells. The mixture can also be used to make chocolate pudding by adding cocoa and skipping the shell.

Connie Hunnicutt Stringer
Tuscaloosa, Alabama

FRUITCAKE COOKIES

1lb mixed candied fruit
1/2 cup flour (plain or self-rising)
Pinch of salt
1 31/2 oz. can coconut
2 cups chopped pecans
1 can sweetened condensed milk

Dredge fruit in flour. Add salt, coconut and nuts.
Add milk and mix thoroughly. Drop by spoonfuls on
greased cookie sheet. Bake 25 - 30 minutes in pre-heated
275 degree oven. Store cooled cookies in an airtight
container about 5 days before serving. Then enjoy!
Makes about 4 dozen.

Gail Estes Hollingsworth

REFRIGERATOR FRUITCAKE

1 can Angel Flake Coconut
1 can Eagle Brand Milk
1 large box Vanilla Wafers
8 oz. red candied cherries
8 oz. green candied cherries
1 qt of pecans, chopped

Crush vanilla wafers into a fine consistency, this can be done in a food processor or blender. Cut cherries into smaller pieces. Mix crushed vanilla wafers with Eagle Brand Milk. Add coconut, cherries and pecans. Form into a log or rectangle using wax paper, cover and refrigerate. Refrigerate overnight or for several hours then slice and enjoy!

Gail Estes Hollingsworth

CRANBERRY SWISS CHEESE BALL

A bit sharp, a bit sweet with a tang. Wonderful on crackers or toasted flat bread squares. 8 oz. Swiss cheese, grated (like Jarlsberg)

4 oz. cream cheese (can use low fat)
3 Tbsp mayonnaise (can use low fat)
¼ tsp. nutmeg
¼ tsp. white pepper
2 tsp. dried lemon zest

With electric mixer or food processor, blend together until creamy. Add ¼ cup chopped dried cranberries and mix in. (Can substitute fresh chopped cranberries, diced maraschino cherries or chopped red and green candied cherries for a holiday look)

Form two balls or one large ball. Wrap in plastic wrap and refrigerate several hours, until firm. Unwrap and roll each ball in chopped pecans or sliced almonds. Wrap balls in plastic wrap. Refrigerate at least one hour before serving. Can be made several days or a week ahead. Keep wrapped. Flavors will enhance with time. *This basic recipe of grated cheese, cream cheese and mayonnaise can be altered to create many yummy cheese balls or spreads. For spreads, use a softer cheese and/or increase mayonnaise to 1/2 cup. Use any kind of cheese and addition of chopped dried fruit or diced peppers, olives and/or spices. For those sensitive to nuts, leave off nuts. Can roll in sunflower seeds, chopped pumpkin seeds

(Pepitas) or chopped peanuts. For a sweet dessert cheese roll, can roll in chocolate sprinkles or red and/or green sugar sprinkles. Great with fresh apple slices or paired with fresh apple cider, sparkling cider, hot-spiced cider, or a favorite wine.

Gail Estes Hollingsworth
Tuscaloosa, Alabama

CHRISTMAS PUNCH

I bottle apple juice or apple cider
I small bag red hot candies
Heat until candy is melted
Serve warm

Kay Finch Swindle

TOMATO PIE

1 can Butter-Me-Not Biscuits
3 Ripe Tomatoes, sliced
1 cup onion, chopped
1 cup bell pepper, chopped
1 stick butter
1 cup mayonnaise
1 cup grated cheddar cheese

Sauté onions and pepper in oleo, set aside Mix mayonnaise and cheese, set aside Roll out 5 biscuits in pie plate for crust. Top with half of onions and pepper, add tomatoes, top with remaining onion mixture. Then cheese mixture. Top with remaining biscuits. Bake at 350 until brown. 8-10 servings. A family favorite!!

Faye Hubbard
Tuscaloosa, Alabama

TURNIP GREEN SOUP

2 10 oz. packages of turnip greens with turnips
1 pkg. Knorr vegetable soup mix
15 oz can navy beans
1 onion, chopped
1lb. smoked sausage, thinly sliced
1 tsp. hot sauce
1 tsp. garlic powder
Salt and pepper to taste
Tony's Seasoning to taste

Pepper sauce to taste Combine all ingredients in soup pot. Bring to a boil and reduce heat to simmer. Cook until onions are tender and sausage is done. Serve with cornbread. This is about as southern as you can get. We usually use fresh turnip greens that Lane grows out by the swimming pool. I freeze leftovers if any.

Faye Hubbard
Tuscaloosa, Alabama

MAGIC COOKIE BARS

1 ½ cups corn flake crumbs
3 T sugar
1 stick melted butter or margarine
1 cup (6oz. pkg.) semi-sweet chocolate morsels
1 1/3 cups (3 ½ oz. can) flaked coconut
1 cup coarsely chopped walnuts
1 can sweetened condensed milk

Mix corn flake crumbs and sugar in 12 x 9 in. baking pan, then add margarine and mix all together. With back of tablespoon, press mixture evenly and firmly in bottom of pan to form crust.

Scatter chocolate morsels over crust. Spread coconut evenly over morsels. Sprinkle walnuts over coconut. Pour sweetened condensed milk evenly over top of layers.

Bake in moderate oven, 350 degrees, about 25 minutes or until lightly browned around edges. Cool. Cut into pieces.

Makes approximately 54 pieces depending on how large piece are cut.

Patsy Bruce
Decatur, Alabama

COCKTAIL MEATBALLS

<u>Meatballs</u>
2 lbs. ground beef
1 cup bread crumbs
2 T instant onions
1 egg
Salt and pepper

Make into 1" meatballs. Cook and drain. These can be made ahead of time and frozen until needed.

<u>Sauce:</u>
Large bottle of grape jelly
Bottle chili sauce

In frying pan, put one large jar of grape jelly and add one bottle of chili sauce. Heat together; add meatballs and coat with sauce.

Serve in a chaffing dish under low heat.
(Recipe says it will make 14 dozen meatballs.
If you make them bigger than 1" it will yield less than that.)

Margo Ross
Milwaukee Wisconsin

VINEGAR BEEF AND SWEET POTATOES

Precook 3 lb. beef roast. Remove fat and shred
Par boil 4 - 6 sweet potatoes in skins until fork
tender. Cool to touch. Skin potatoes and slice into thick
slices lengthwise.
Layer meat and potatoes in large Pyrex casserole
dish.

Vinegar Sauce
1 cup water
1/2 cup apple cider vinegar
1/2 box brown sugar
1 cup granulated sugar
black pepper
1 stick butter
1/2 bottle barbecue sauce
(Any brand will do)

Preheat oven to 350 degrees
Pour 3/4 of vinegar sauce into casserole dish over
roast and potatoes. Bake for about 45 minutes and baste
with remaining sauce every 15 minutes.

Hope you will be able to include this recipe, as it is a
family favorite.

Love,
Joan Smithson
Tuscaloosa, Alabama

More by Beth Albirght

In Dixie Series:

Magic In Dixie (Book One)

Christmas In Dixie (Book Two)

Daydreams In Dixie (Book Three)

Stardust in Dixie (Book Four)

A Christmas Wedding in Dixie (Book Five)

The Sassy Belles Series:

The Sassy Belles

Wedding Belles

Sleigh Belles

Saved By The Belles

Memoirs

Southern Exposure; Tales From My Front Porch

Meet Beth Albright

 Beth Albright is a Tuscaloosa native, former Days Of Our Lives actress, and former radio and TV talk show host. She is a graduate of the University Of Alabama School of Journalism. She is also a screenwriter, voice-over artist, wife of her college sweetheart, Ted and mother of her favorite person on earth, her brilliant handsome son, Brooks. A perpetually homesick Southern Belle and a major Alabama Crimson Tide fan, she splits her time between the tiny historic hamlet of Cedarburg, Wisconsin and, of course, Tuscaloosa.

Beth loves to connect with her readers.

Visit her online:
www.bethalbrightbooks.com

Facebook:
https://www.facebook.com/authorbethalbright

Twitter:
https://twitter.com/BeththeBelle

Goodreads:
https://www.goodreads.com/author/show/
6583748.Beth_Albright

42999038R00099

Made in the USA
Middletown, DE
28 April 2017